Ernest B. Bax

The Story of the French Revolution

Second Edition

Ernest B. Bax

The Story of the French Revolution
Second Edition

ISBN/EAN: 9783337227500

Printed in Europe, USA, Canada, Australia, Japan

Cover: Foto ©Andreas Hilbeck / pixelio.de

More available books at **www.hansebooks.com**

THE STORY OF
THE FRENCH REVOLUTION

BY

E. BELFORT BAX

AUTHOR OF " THE RELIGION OF SOCIALISM," " THE ETHICS OF SOCIALISM,"
" JEAN PAUL MARAT," ETC.

SECOND EDITION.

LONDON

SWAN SONNENSCHEIN & CO.
PATERNOSTER SQUARE
1892

PREFACE TO THE SECOND EDITION.

THE acceptance by the Public of the First Edition of this Book seems to show that the anticipated want for a condensed sketch of the history of the French Revolution—more especially from a point of view from which it has not hitherto been treated, except, perhaps, in isolated monographs—was a real one. With a view of making this Second Edition still more worthy, it has been revised throughout; certain portions having been completely recast, and a few slight errors, which had crept into the book, corrected.

E. B. B.

PREFACE.

THE following sketch of the course of the French Revolution was originally published during 1889 in serial form in "Justice," the weekly organ of the Social Democratic Federation. It has been revised, corrected, and, in some parts, added to, for the present re-issue. It need scarcely be said that it in no way pretends to be a complete history of the great political, social, and intellectual movement it describes. The present volume is designed primarily as a guide to those who, not having the time to study larger works on the subject, yet wish during these centennial years to have in a small compass a connected description of the main events of the French Revolution, more especially from the point of view of modern Socialism. It is undeniable that there are many Englishmen who would indignantly repudiate any aspersions on their education for whom the French Revolution means little more than the destruction of one institution called the Bastille, the erection of another institution called the Guillotine, and the establishment of the Napoleonic Empire on the ruins of both. They have no idea of the complex forces, economical, speculative, and political, which manifested themselves in the succession of crises (scarcely, indeed, of the existence of the crises themselves) which took place between the assembling of the States-General in 1789, and the suppression of the Babœuf conspiracy in 1796.

For such as these, and for many others to whom the above remarks will not altogether apply, a condensed statement of the facts of the French Revolution cannot but be desirable,

and although there exist summaries galore, the writer ventures
to think that the present little work differs from them in two
respects : firstly, in the point of view from which the Revolution
is viewed, and secondly, in the endeavour to throw the principal
events into as strong relief as possible by the omission of all
detail which is unessential to the understanding of them.
Brevity has also been a distinct aim, and for this, as for the
former reason, much that is in itself interesting has been left
out. The foregoing especially applies to biographical details
respecting the chief actors. These have been uniformly omitted
throughout, as tending to expand the sketch indefinitely, and
to draw off attention from its main purpose. The circumstances
of the time and the events made the personalities what they
were, and there is not one of them who, in so far as public
life is concerned, can be regarded otherwise than as the embodiment of some more or less wide-spread contemporary
tendency. The actors, therefore, merely cross the stage in
connection with the principal events in which they played a
rôle. Yet, though they may have suddenly become especially
prominent, it must be understood that, in almost all cases,
they were already familiar to the population of Paris, and, in
many cases, of the whole of France, as club-orators, parliamentary politicians, or as journalists. It is not too much to
say that in the French Revolution journalism first became a
power in the world's history.

Those who seek further details both of the Revolution itself
and of the life of its leading figures may be referred to the
larger histories. The admirable history of Mr. Morse Stephen
now in progress represents by far the best work that has as yet
been done in English (both as regards exhaustiveness and im-
partiality) in connection with the subject. Mr. Stephen's
excellent articles in the ninth edition of the "Encyclopædia
Britannica" may also be consulted with profit. The French

literature of the subject would, of course, fill libraries. Works such as Bougeart's "Marat," Avenel's "Anacharsis Clootz," are monuments of industry in research. In spite of the efforts of French scholars, however, there is much room left for original investigation. The British Museum alone contains, I believe, upwards of 100,000 newspapers, pamphlets, manifestoes, and other documents, many of them as yet unarranged and un-catalogued. The amount of material in Paris, and in France generally, which has not yet been worked is probably incalcul-able.

Offence has been given in some quarters at the view taken of Robespierre in the following pages. The writer can only say that he cannot regard the mere negative qualification that Robespierre has been in general attacked by the Reaction in conjunction with other leaders as of itself entitling him to the esteem of modern Democrats or Socialists in the teeth of the undeniable facts of the case. The treacherous surrender of the Dantonists, the judicial murder of the Hébertists, the law of Prairial, are these things not written in history? The fact is, Robespierre was a *petit bourgeois*, a Philistine to the backbone, who desired a Republic of *petit bourgeois* virtues, with himself at the head, and was prepared to wade through a sea of blood for the accomplishment of his end. Napoleon had a truer sense of the case than other Reactionists, when, as is reported, he was inclined to hail Robespierre as an unsuccessful predecessor in the work of "restoring order" and "saving society"—in the interest, of course, of the middle-classes. With these few words of preface the volume is left to the consideration of the reader, in the hope that it may afford him at least some light on the general bearings of the history of the French Revolu-tion.

THE STORY OF THE FRENCH REVOLUTION.

CHAPTER I.

THE LITERARY PROLOGUE.

THE cardinal idea of the French Revolution was the political emancipation of the middle-class. The feudal hierarchy of the Middle Ages consisted in France, as in other countries, of three main social divisions, or estates, as they were termed, (1) The superior territorial clergy, (2) the nobles, and (3) the smaller landholders, the free tenants, and the citizens of the independent townships. The mere serf or villein (holding by servile tenure), or common labourer, was like the slave of antiquity, un-classified. The possession or (non-servile) tenure of land was the condition of freedom. This third estate was the germ of our middle-class. The great problem of the French Revolution, then, was to obtain the independence and domination of the third estate. It is expressed in the words of its representative, the Abbé Siéyès : " What are we of the third estate ? Nothing. What would we be ? Everything." But, although the political suprem-acy of the middle-class was the central idea, and the one which it realised (thereby effectually refuting a certain order of politicians that declares violent revolutions to be necessarily abortive), there were issues raised—and not merely raised, but carried for the time being—which

A

went far beyond this. But the flood-tide of the Revolution did not represent the permanent gain of progress. The waters receded from the ground touched at the height of the crisis, leaving the enfranchisement of the bourgeoisie as the one achievement permanently effected.

Foremost among the precursors of this mighty change was the Genevese thinker, Jean Jacques Rousseau (1712—1778). This remarkable personality may be termed the Messiah of the Revolutionary Crisis. His writings were quoted and read as a new gospel by well-nigh all the prominent leaders of the time. Rousseau's doctrines were contained in an early essay on civilisation, in his "Emile, a Treatise on Education," and in the "Contrat Social," his chief work.

In his first essay, Rousseau maintained the superiority of the savage over the civilised state, and the whole of his subsequent teaching centred in deprecation of the hollowness and artificiality of society, and in an inculcation of the imperative need of a return, as far as might be, to a state of nature in all our relations. This he especially applies to education in his "Emile," in which he sketches the training of a hypothetical child.

The "Social Contract," his greatest work, contains a discussion of the first principles of social and political order. It is to this work the magic formulas which served as watchwords during the Revolution, formulas such as "Liberty, Equality, and Fraternity," "Divine Right of Insurrection," the term "Citizen," employed as a style of address, and many other things are traceable. The title of the work was suggested by Locke's (or rather Hobbes') supposition of a primitive contract having been entered into between governor and governed, which was set up in opposition to that of the "divine right" of kings. This idea Rousseau accepts in basis, but denies the unconditional nature of the contract affirmed by the originators of the theory. No original distinction existed between rulers and ruled. Any contract of the kind that obtained was merely a political convenience strictly subject to conditions. Governors were merely the delegates or mandatories of the people. The form of government was to Rousseau more or less a minor matter. Although a democracy had the most advantages, yet it was quite possible for the mandates of the people to be adequately carried out by a special body of men (an aristocracy), or even by one man (a king). But every form of government was bound to recognise the will of the people as sovereign in all things.

The classicism of the French Revolution is also largely represented in Rousseau. The Roman constitution is invariably the source of his illustrations and the model to be copied or amended. As regards toleration, Rousseau would allow the civil power the right of suppressing views which were deemed contrary to good citizenship. Like the Romans, he would tolerate all religions equally that did not menace the State. There is probably no single book that has produced such stupendous results within a few years, if at all, as Rousseau's "Social Contract." It is the text-book of the French Revolution. Every ordinance, every law, every draft of constitution bears the mark of its influence. Although more logical in the working-out of the theory than its founders, it is needless to say that Rousseau's own views are singularly barren and unhistorical, as every theory must be that deals only with the political side of things. One may admire his loathing at the artificiality of the world around him, at the " organised hypocrisy " called religion and morality ; but in his day it was impossible to uncover its historical roots, and hence, to modern ears, his diatribes lose much of their effect.

The influence of the second of the important precursors of the French Revolution, Francois-Marie Arouet de Voltaire (1694-1778), was much more indirect than that of Rousseau. Voltaire's influence was almost purely negative. By his wit he scorched up all the reverence remaining in the minds of men for the forms of the old, outworn Feudal-Catholic organisation. Though there was a great amount of adroit self-seeking in Voltaire's character, it is as impossible to deny that there was also much that was genuine and truly noble in his indignation at cruelty and his detestation of Christian hypocrisy, as that it produced a far-reaching effect on the events that followed. Voltaire, although personally a Frenchman of Frenchmen, breathes the spirit of a conscious cosmopolitanism and contempt for nationality in his writings, which for the first time in history became a popular creed during the Revolution, and was expressed in the famous appeal of 1793.

But in this, as in other respects, Voltaire was not alone. He partly created and partly reflected the prevalent tone of the French *salon* culture of the eighteenth century. This, if we cared to do so, we might trace back in its main features to the revival of learning—to the courts of the Medicis. And here it may be well to remind our readers, in passing, of the truth that individual genius merely means the special faculty of expressing that so-called " spirit of the age " to which that of preceding ages has led up ; and that Voltaire and Rousseau merely achieved the results they did by reason of their capacity for reproducing in words the shapeless thoughts of millions. To this, in the case of Voltaire, must be added a special width of intellectual sympathy which took in an unusually large number of different subjects.

Besides Rousseau and Voltaire, we must not omit to mention the brilliant group of contemporary workers and thinkers, headed by Diderot and D'Alembert, who built up that monument of laborious industry, the great French Encyclopædia. Immense difficulties attended the publication of this important work, notwithstanding that care was taken to exclude any expressions of overt contempt or hostility towards current prejudices. Again, we must not forget the Materialist-Atheists, central among whom was Baron d'Holbach, the anonymous author of the celebrated "System of Nature," a book which, though crude according to modern notions, did good work in its day—work which a treatise of more intrinsic philosophical value probably would not have achieved. It is noteworthy that most of the other prominent names among the pre-revolutionary writers, including Rousseau and Voltaire, are those of ardent deists. The name of Montesquieu (1689-1755), whose " Esprit des Lois " was a text-book of juridical philosophy for the Revolution, must also not be omitted from the list of its literary precursors.

All these men contributed their share in preparing the mental foundation for the great upheaval which followed. It is strange, however, that not one of them lived to see the practical issue of his labours. Rousseau, the most directly powerful of them, died eleven years before the taking of the Bastille, and Voltaire the same year. Diderot lived till 1784; D'Alembert died the previous year; Mirabeau, alone of all who had prepared the great crisis, lived to see its beginning. But even he succumbed in 1791, a year and a half before the actual fall of the monarchy. Few of these men saw more than a free-thinking aristocracy and literary class. Of the movement below they recked little, scarcely perhaps that there was such a movement. For although from the beginning of the century, notably throughout the reign of Louis XV., there was ever and anon the consciousness of a change as imminent, and although twice, in 1734 and in 1771, the old system seemed on the point of breaking down in revolution, yet still it survived, and for aught men could tell, was destined to continue to survive many more such shocks. The throne, therefore, doubtless to many, seemed as secure, religion as popular, as ever, the same throne and the same religion which in a few years were destined to be involved in so mighty an overthrow.

CHAPTER II.

THE ECONOMIC PRELUDE IN THE PROVINCES.

TEN years of bad harvests, aggravated by an effete industrial, fiscal, and political system, culminated with the summer of 1788. A great drought was succeeded by a violent hailstorm, which dealt destruction all round. The harvest was worse than ever before. All kinds of agricultural crops failed miserably all over France, not alone wheat and grain generally, but vines, chestnuts, olives, in short, all the natural products of consumption and exportation. Even what was gathered in was so spoiled as to be almost unfit for use. From every province of France came the monotonous tale of ruin, famine, starvation. Even the comparatively well-to-do peasant farmer could obtain nothing but barley bread of a bad quality, and water, while the less well-off had to put up with bread made from dried hay or moistened chaff, which we are told "caused the death of many children." The Englishman, Arthur Young, who was travelling through France this year, wherever he went heard nothing but the story of the distress of the people and the dearness of bread. "Such bread as is to be obtained tastes of mould, and often produces dysentery and other diseases. The larger towns present the same condition, as though they had undergone the extremities of a long siege. In some places the whole store of corn and barley has the stench of putrefaction, and is full of maggots." To add to the horrors of the situation, upon the hot and dry summer followed a winter of unparalled severity. The new year of 1789 opened with the Seine frozen over from Paris to Havre. No such weather had been experienced since 1709. As the spring advanced the misery increased. The industrial crisis became acute in the towns, thousands of workmen were thrown out of employment owing to the introduction of recently invented machinery from England, which was beginning to supersede hand-labour in some trades. The riots and local disturbances which had for many years past been taking place sporadically in various districts, now became daily more frequent, so much so that from March onwards the whole peasantry of France may be said to have been in a state of open insurrection, three hundred separate risings in the provinces being counted for the four months preceding the taking of the Bastille.

In 1787, the Minister Lomenie de Brienne had created nineteen new provincial assemblies. Below the arrondissement, or district assembly, which had been instituted some years before, now came the assembly of the parish. In each of these primary assemblies of the parish, the arrondisement, and even of the province, the "people, farmers, &c., sat side by side with the local dignitaries," a fact which, as may be imagined, considerably tended to obliterate the ancient feudal awe. In November, 1787, the King announced his intention of convoking the States-General. On the 5th of July, 1788, the various local bodies were called upon to draw up *cahiers*, or statements of their grievances, for presentment before the King and States-General, in which a double representation of the "third estate" was conceded. These *cahiers* form a mass of the most interesting material illustrative of the condition of France just before the Revolution, and have not even yet been fully investigated. "The King," said the proclamation, "desires that from the extremities of his kingdom, and the least known of its habitations, each may feel assurance in bringing before him his views and grievances," and this and other similar expressions were interpreted by the peasantry in the natural sense that the King was really desirous of rescuing them from starvation. It accordingly emboldened them to take the matter into their own hands. In January the *cahiers* were drawn up, which meant that the people had now for the first time formulated their ills. Discussion in the assemblies had excited them. The States-General was going to look to their wrongs, it was true, but the States-General did not meet till May, and meanwhile they were starving. One thing was clear, they must have bread. Accordingly, in defiance of local authorities and guardians of the peace, bands ranging up to three or four hundred and more formed themselves all over France, seized and plundered granaries, religious houses, stores of all kinds, entered public buildings in the name of the people, destroying all legal documents (justly regarded as the instruments of their servitude) which they could lay their hands on, proclaimed the local dues and taxes abolished, summarily put to death all those who interfered with them in the name of law and order, and, emboldened by success, finally took to the burning of the chateaux and the indiscriminate destruction and appropriation of the houses and property of the wealthy. That the numbers of these bands were augmented not only by the workmen out of employment in Paris, Rouen, &c., but also by professional thieves, was only to be expected. The local authorities were hopelessly inadequate to cope with the insurgents, the central authority in Paris seemed paralysed.

Ordinary readers of the history of the Revolution are apt to forget, in following the course of events in the metropolis, that they were only an enlarged picture of what was going on in hundreds of towns and villages throughout the provinces. Both before and after the famous 14th of July, in most of the provinces of France all constituted authority was at an end. No one durst disobey the mandates of the popular insurgents. It would be impossible, and tedious if it were possible, to

enumerate all the circumstances of these
revolts. The manner was pretty much the same in all,
and the following account of an insurrection at Stras-
burg may serve to illustrate it. Five or six hundred
peasants, artisans, unemployed, tramps, and others, seize
the occasion of a public holiday to attack the Hotel de
Ville, the assembled magistrates escaping precipitately
by back doors. The windows disappear under a volley
of stones, the doors are broken in with crowbars, and the
crowd enters like a torrent. "Immediately," the account
states, "there was a rain of shutters, window-sashes,
chairs, tables, sofas, books, papers, &c." The public
archives are thrown to the winds, the neighbouring
streets being covered with them. Deeds, charters, &c.,
perish in the flames. In the cellars, tuns containing
valuable wines are forced, the marauders, after drinking
their fill, allowing them to run until there is a pond
formed five feet deep, in which several people are
drowned. Others, loaded with booty, run off with it
under the eyes of the soldiers, who rather encourage the
proceedings than otherwise. For three whole days the
city is given over to the mob. All the houses belonging
to persons of local distinction are sacked from cellar to
attic. The revolt spreads instantly throughout the
neighbouring country. (Taine, "Origines," tom i. pp.
81-82.)

A few weeks before the opening of the States-
General a great riot occurred in Paris, in the Faubourg
St. Antoine, the workmen's quarter, attended by much
bloodshed and loss of life. Paris, we are told, had for
months past begun to fill with desperate, hungry, and
ragged strangers drawn thither by poverty from the
uttermost ends of France.

In some districts the leaders pretend to be acting
under the orders of the King. The result is everywhere
at least one thing,—the enforcement of a *maximum*
in the price of bread, and the abolition of taxes. Atroci-

that the King w—— ——here and there. A lawyer is half-starved to make him surrender a charter supposed to be in his possession; a lord is tortured to death; an ecclesiastic torn in pieces. Thus have threatened ruin and starvation, to which the financial extravagances of the Court have been the occasion of giving articulate expression, and the remedy for which is offered, to those who can read, in the "Social Contract" of Rousseau, become the immediate cause of the French Revolution. The same imminent bankruptcy of the kingdom occasioned by the extravagance of the Court which led to the convocation of the States-General, led also indirectly to the founding of that main-spring of the Revolution, the Jacobins' Club. The dispute between the Court and the local legal Councils, called "Parliaments," led to the crippling of their powers by the King, and this again, to remonstrant deputations from the aggrieved provincial towns. One set of these remonstrants, hailing from Rennes, in Brittany, formed themselves into a club called the Breton Club, for the ventilation of their grievances, using the old Convent of St. Jacques in the Rue St. Honoré for their meetings. The original scope of the society soon became enlarged, and the name changed from that of Breton Club to Jacobins' Club, after their meeting-place. Such was the origin of the vast club-organisation, which exercised such a stupendous influence not only in Paris, but in all France, during the following years.

CHAPTER III.

THE OPENING IN PARIS.

On the 5th of May, 1789, the royal town of Versailles was gay—gay with decorations, with music, vocal and instrumental, with epaulettes, "etiquettes," fair women, and fair costumes. It was the opening of the States-General, called together for the first time since 1614, as a last resource to rescue the realm from dissolution and impending bankruptcy—and also *the definitive opening of the French Revolution.*

At midday might have been seen the feudal procession entering the Church of St. Louis. After the King and Royal Family, the clergy occupied the first place, "the superior clergy," attired in purple robe and lawn sleeves; the less "superior," in cassock, cloak, and square bonnet. Next came the nobles, habited in black, with silver-faced vest, lace cravat, and plumed hat; while bringing up the rear followed the humble *tiers-état*—the representatives of the middle-class, the merchants, the farmers, and the small landowners—dressed also in black, but adorned with merely a short cloak and plain hat. With this memorable procession, the constitution of the Middle Ages, moribund for over two centuries, spasmodically gasped its last breath.

The business of the States-General did not pass off as gaily as the opening ceremony. Conflict between the orders followed immediately, on points of procedure, with the result that the third estate constituted itself the National Assembly of France, refusing to admit the other orders to its deliberations except on a basis of

equality.   The King manifested his displeasure by closing
the door of the hall of the States against them.   The Assembly answered by the celebrated oath it took outside
in the Tennis Court of Versailles, 20th June, by which it
pledged itself not to separate until it had given France a
Constitution.   The Assembly triumphed over the Court
two days after its oath, inasmuch as it regained possession of its hall, openly defied the King in person, abolished
the independence of the clergy and noblesse, formally
confirmed its decrees of the previous day which the King
had quashed, and proceeded with its deliberations.   Thus
the curtain rose on the first act of the revolutionary
drama.

Meanwhile the new popular ferment occasioned by the
events at Versailles had taken complete possession of
the capital, and was rapidly spreading into the provinces.
Some weeks later, early in July, Necker, the Minister of
Finance, beloved by the middle-class, was dismissed from
office.   Necker, it should be observed, was one of the less
bad of the scoundrels, called finance ministers, who have
been malversating the national funds in succession for
years past.   By comparison he appeared almost virtuous,
and the populace, whose charity and admiration are
always boundless toward official personages, when not
quite so bad as one would expect, had converted him into
an object of adoration.   A procession for the purpose of
protesting against the minister's dismissal was dispersed
by force of arms and two persons killed.   The city was
soon in uproar.   The Palais-Royal, the great place of
public assembly and political discussion, was packed with
over ten thousand persons.   On the table, which served
for a tribune, stood a young man, of fine features and
gentle mien, who was haranguing the crowd.   It was
Camille Desmoulins, the popular journalist.   " Citizens,"
said he, " there is not a moment to lose !   The removal of
Necker is the tocsin for a St. Bartholomew of patriots !
This evening, all the Swiss and German battalions are

coming from the Champ de Mars to slaughter us! There remains but one resource; let us rush to arms!" So saying, he placed in his hat a sprig of a tree—green being the emblem of hope. The example was followed till the chestnut trees of Paris were denuded. At the same time the tricolour flag was first adopted as the banner of the popular party.

The crowd proceeded through the streets, bearing in triumph the busts of Necker and Philippe Egalité, the King's cousin but not his friend, its numerical strength increasing with every yard traversed, till its course was arrested on the Pont-Royal by a detachment of the Royal German Cavalry. The latter were driven back by showers of stones, and the concourse swept onwards as far as the Place Louis XV. Here a formidable street fight took place, the people being opposed by a squadron of dragoons. The regulars of the King, after encountering a vigorous resistance, at length routed the insurgent Parisians, but the victory was more fatal to the cause they represented than any defeat could have been. The dispersed multitude carried the indignant cry, "To arms!" from end to end of Paris. The regiment of French Guards quartered in Paris mutinied, and put to flight the mercenary foreign troops intended to overawe them.

The whole night long the tocsin rang out from the Hotel de Ville, where a committee of prominent citizens was sitting to organise a search for arms. The morning of the 12th July saw Paris in full revolt; the tocsins of all the churches were pealing; drums were beating along all the main streets; excited crowds collecting in every opening space; an influx of the "disinherited" class trooped in at all the gates of Paris; gunsmiths' shops were ransacked; on all sides a mad search for weapons was the order of the day. The Committee at the Hotel de Ville, in response to the importunate demands for arms, could only reply that they had none. The civic authorities, next appealed to, temporised and evasively promised assistance. Houses were sacked; carriages seized. In the confusion there were naturally not wanting ruffians who sought to make use of the state of things prevailing for purposes of mere plunder. Such excesses were peremptorily put down with the cry, "Death to the thieves." The equipages and other property of the "aristocrats" when seized by the people were always either destroyed or carried to a central station at the Place de Grêve. In the afternoon "the provost of the merchants" (a dignitary of the effete mediæval hierarchy corresponding to the modern *maire*) announced the speedy arrival of the muskets and ammunition so eagerly clamoured for on all sides. A citizen militia was formed under the name of the Parisian Guard, numbering 48,000 men; cockades of red, blue, and green were everywhere distributed; but the hours passed on and no muskets arrived. A panic seized the city that the mercenary troops were about to march on Paris during the ensuing night. At last chests purporting to contain ammunition did appear, were eagerly torn open, and found to contain—old linen and broken pieces of wood!

The Committee men and the "provost of the merchants" alike narrowly escaped with their lives. But the provost, pleading that he had been himself deceived, tried to divert the attention of the people by sending them on a futile expedition to Chartreux. The Committee finally hit upon the device of arming the citizens with pikes, in default of firearms, and accordingly ordered 50,000 to be forged. As a measure of protection against thieves and plunderers, the city was illuminated throughout the night.

CHAPTER IV.

THE BASTILLE.

Next morning (the 14th) early, the word was passed among the populace, "To the Invalides!" the military hospital. There at least arms must be forthcoming. And sure enough the people were rewarded for their courage in braving the troops assembled in the Champ de Mars, and forcing their way into the great military depot.

Twenty-eight thousand muskets, besides cannon, sabres, and spears were carried off in triumph. Meanwhile the alarm had been given that the royal regiments, posted at St. Denis, were on the way to the capital, and, above all, that the cannon of the Bastille itself was pointed toward the boulevard St. Antoine.

The attention of Paris was at once directed to the former point, which really commanded the most populous districts of the city. The whole morning there was but one cry, "To the Bastille!" The Bastille was the great emblem of the King's authority. In the middle ages it had been the Royal stronghold against the turbulent feudal barons. But though the French nobility had long ceased to be "turbulent barons" and had become obsequious courtiers, the Bastille remained, nevertheless, the great visible embodiment of the, at present, long centralised authority of the King of France. The capture of the Bastille would therefore be the greatest blow the King's *prestige* could possibly suffer. Add to this, that although no longer employed for its original purpose, the Bastille had become specially obnoxious, owing to its use as a place for arbitrary imprisonment under the infamous *lettres de cachets*. Armed crowds assembled then at this place from all quarters, till the great fortress seemed confronted by the whole city in arms. Negotiations took place with the governor, Delaunay, but the people persistently shouted, "We want the Bastille!" The die was cast by the destruction of the great bridge, which was battered down by blows from hatchets, it is said, by two men only. The concourse poured in; the second drawbridge was attacked and vigorously defended by the small garrison.

Numbers of the assailants fell, killed and wounded. The siege continued over four hours, when the French Guard, who, as we have seen, had already sided with the Revolution, arrived with cannon. The garrison, seeing the case hopeless, themselves urged the governor to surrender. But old Delaunay preferred blowing the place up and burying himself amidst the ruins. His companions alone prevented him from carrying out this design. The soldiers thereupon surrendered on condition that their lives should be spared. The leaders of the people who were in the forefront, and had given their word to this effect, did their utmost to protect the garrison from the indignation of the crowd. But among the thousands that thronged in there were probably few who knew anything of what had taken place. As a consequence, Delaunay and some of the Swiss garrison fell victims to the popular fury.

Meanwhile the Hotel de Ville was in trepidation. Above all, the "provost of the merchants," Flesselles, trembled lest he should be made to suffer for his treachery. These fears were not allayed when shouts of "Victory!" "Liberty!" issuing from thousands of throats, assailed the ears of the inmates, and grew louder minute by minute. It was the conquerors of the Bastille carrying their heroes in triumph to the municipal head-quarters.

Presently there entered the great hall, an enthusiastic, but disorderly, ragged, and bloodstained crowd, promiscuously armed with pikes, muskets, hatchets, and well-nigh every other conceivable weapon. Above the heads of the crowd one held the keys of the Bastille, another the "regulations" of the prison, a third the collar of the governor.

A general amnesty for all the defenders captured was agreed to after much opposition. But the "provost of the merchants" did not get off so easily. On the corpse of Delaunay a letter had been found, in which Flesselles had stated that he was amusing the Parisians with cockades and promises, and that if the fortress could only hold out till nightfall relief should come. A Court was to have been improvised in the Palais Royal to judge him, but on the way thither he was laid dead by a pistol-shot from one of the crowd.

The excitement of the day's action over, precautions to avert designs against the capital on the part of the Court were redoubled. Everywhere barricades were raised, paving stones torn up, pikes forged. The whole population was all night long at work in the streets. How well-grounded were the fears of the Parisians would have been evident to anyone behind the scenes at Versailles, where Breteuil, the prime minister, had just promised the King to restore the royal authority in three days, this very night having been fixed for the expedition, and wine and presents distributed among the royal troops in anticipation.

The Assembly, which was sitting *en permanence*, was about to send one more deputation to the King (it had already sent two) when he appeared in person in its midst. On being informed during the night of the events that had taken place, by the "Grand Master of the Wardrobe," he exclaimed "It is a revolt." "No, sire," replied the Grand Master, "It is a revolution." On the King's subsequent protestations of affection for his subjects, and his statement that he had just given orders for the withdrawal of the foreign troops from Paris and Versailles, that he confided his person to the representatives of the nation alone, &c., the Assembly gave way to

B

transports of joy, rose *en masse*, and escorted him to the palace.

The news spread rapidly. A revulsion of feeling took place all round, from terror to elation, from hatred to gratitude. The general jubilation was increased by the restoration of Necker, the entry of Louis XVI. into Paris, and his acceptance of the tricolour cockade. Thus ended the preparatory period of the Revolution. It is needless to say the moral effect of the popular victory throughout France was immense, every town becoming henceforth a revolutionary centre in the sense of possessing a definite revolutionary organisation.

There are one or two useful hints to be learned from this old and oft-repeated story of the fall of the Bastille. The first is of the eminent utility of popular "force" if only applied at the right moment. Beforehand, it would have seemed preposterous that "an undisciplined mob" could take a fortress and paralyse the efforts of a reaction possessed of a trained army. Yet so it was.

Another point to note is the untrustworthiness of men who belong to the class which makes the revolution, and who even profess to represent it, when their personal interest and position are bound up with the maintenance of the existing order. Flesselles, a man of the third estate, its leading dignitary in the city of Paris, was yet the man who was the least anxious to see the feudal hierarchy overthrown. And why? Because he played a part in it. The "third estate" had been incorporated into the mediæval system. He was its representative as one of the feudal orders. Its position was subordinate indeed, but, now that it was growing in importance, its leading men had much more to gain by clinging to the skirts of the *noblesse*, and aiding them in frustrating that complete revolution which the rank and file of the class were seeking, than in assisting the accomplishment of this revolution, which could only mean the effacement of their own personal position. History repeats itself. Trades unions have

won for themselves recognition and patronage in the
middle-class world to-day. Their leaders, in a similar
way, do not exhibit any special desire for a change which,
though it would mean the liberation and triumph of the
class they represent, would, at the same time, render
trades unions a thing of the past, no less than the lord
mayors and cabinet ministers who stroke the backs of the
parliamentary elect of trades unions. No, verily, this is
not a nice prospect for the trades union leaders !

CHAPTER V.

THE CONSTITUTION MONGERS.

THE Constitution was now in full train. The Revolution up to the latter point was officially recognised.

There was no harking back for any one. Foulon and Berthier, two "administrators of the first rank," under the old regime, had been publicly hanged, *à la lanterne*, and quartered by the people. The first stratum of revolutionists was to the fore. Mirabeau, Lafayette, and Bailly are the central figures of the Constituent Assembly. Duport, Barnave, and Lameth its extreme men. The Comte de Mirabeau (1749-1791), one of the pre-revolutionary writers, was the leader of the Moderate party in the Assembly. His stupendous powers of oratory made him a useful ally and a dangerous foe. This the Court was not slow in discovering, and accordingly Mirabeau was soon won over by bribes to do his best to frustrate every popular measure in the Assembly, while all the time professing devotion to the cause of liberty and the people. When this failed, the popular (?) orator did not disdain to resort to actual plotting.

The Marquis de Lafayette (1757-1834), of American Independence notoriety, another member of the noblesse, who had adopted previously to the Revolution the quasi-advanced views then fashionable with his class, was the military representative of the Moderate party in his capacity of commandant of the National Guard, besides the henchman of Mirabeau in the Assembly. Bailly (1736-1793), who was elected Mayor of Paris the day after the taking of the Bastille, also coadjutated in the work.

of moderating the Revolution alike in his official capacity and in the Assembly. As to the extreme men, they really represented but the most moderate form of constitutional monarchy. The situation of parties may be estimated by the fact that Barnave advocated a suspensory veto on the part of the King, while Mirabeau strenuously supported the absolute veto. And be it remembered at such a time, the right of vetoing obnoxious measures would have been no mere matter of form. It appears, then, that even the most advanced Parliament-arians of the day were not prepared to go beyond the present Prussian Constitution. Nevertheless, circum-stances early forced upon this timid and comparatively re-actionary Assembly some drastic political measures, first and foremost on the memorable night of the 4th of August, the abolition of all seignorial rights and privi-leges. At a later stage after the assembly had removed to Paris, a little judicious coercion from the tribunes, or people's galleries, which were tenanted by advanced revolutionists, there is no doubt exercised a salutary influence on several occasions. The members knew well enough that their lives were in the hands of the Paris populace, and those of their wives and children, besides their property, at the mercy of the populace of the rural districts.

The Assembly's first important performance after the fall of the Bastille was the declaration of the Rights of Man, in imitation of the Americans after the successful termination of the War of Independence. The declara-tion of the Rights of Man contains a series of articles, laying down the principles of political equality. Most of them are unexceptionable and even trite, but it is significant that number 17 affirms, categorically,. the absolute sacredness of private property. The question which arose immediately subsequent to this, on the constitution of the Chamber and its relations to the King, need not detain us. It is sufficient to state that while the Assembly was amusing itself discussing "suspensory veto," or "absolute veto," the Court, viz., Queen and Company at Versailles, were meditating the transference of the King to Metz, where the mercenary German troops were stationed, and whence communication with the French noblesse who had emigrated, and the reactionary foreign powers, was easy, the idea being to declare Paris and the Assembly rebels, and march upon the city with the view of restoring the absolute monarchy. These machinations at Versailles are interesting as having given the direction to the first great demonstration of the proletariat of Paris during the Revolution. I say the direction, as the proximate cause was the advice, the now rising popular journalist, Marat, had given some days before in his *Ami du Peuple*, when discussing the scarcity of bread.

The revolt broke out in this way. A woman beating a drum patrolled the streets, crying, "Bread! bread!" She was soon surrounded by large numbers of women, who repaired to the Hotel de Ville demanding bread and arms, at the same time raising the cry, "To Versailles!" which was taken up by the populace generally, with the suddenness characteristic of Parisian outbreaks. The National Guard and the French Guard eventually joined in, with such persistence and unanimity, that Lafayette, after some hours of expostulation, was compelled to place himself at their head, the troops having begun to march without him.

The unexpected appearance of a concourse headed by women and backed by a large armed force, naturally threw the Queen and Court into a state of "amazement and admiration" (in the Shaksperean sense). The household troops at once surrounded the palace. The women, however, expressed peaceable intentions, and through their spokeswoman laid their grievances before the King and the Assembly, describing the direness of the famine prevailing. Meanwhile, in the courtyard of the palace, which was filled with a motley crowd, a quarrel arose, an officer of the King's troops having struck a National Guard. This was the signal for an immediate conflict between the two armed bodies. The people and the Nationals were furious, and the collision must have resulted in more bloodshed than it did, had it not been for the darkness of the night, and the prudent order given the Royal soldiers to cease from firing and to retreat.

The disturbance was eventually quelled, the crowds melting away gradually as the night advanced. The royal family retired to rest at two o'clock; Lafayette, who had remained up all night, in vain endeavoured to snatch repose for an hour at five a.m. Before six, some members of the previous evening's crowd who had remained at Versailles, insulted one of the body-guard, who drew upon them, wounding one of their number. The sleepless "hero of two worlds" (so-called from his American adventures) was soon upon the scene; he found considerable remnants of yesterday's gathering furiously forcing their way into the palace. The assailants were temporarily dispersed, but soon reassembled clamouring for the King. The King eventually appeared upon the balcony, promising, in reply to the popular demands, that he would go to Paris with his family.

The Queen, the head and front of all the recent offending, next stepped on the balcony in the company of the arch-courtier Lafayette, who with a profound obeisance kissed the hand of the woman who had been plotting the massacre of that very people for whom this hypocritical charlatan had been all along professing zeal and devotion. But the humiliation of the Parisians was not yet ended. Lafayette retiring, re-appeared with one of the obnoxious body-guard, and placing the tricolour cockade upon his breast embraced him. At each of these points the assembled crowd duly cheered. The royal family then set out for Paris, and the Tuileries became henceforth their permanent residence.

CHAPTER VI.

THE NEW CONSTITUTION.

AFTER the events we have just described, which occurred on the 5th and 6th of October, 1789, the course of the Revolution was, for some considerable time, peaceful and parliamentary. The Assembly, till then at Versailles, soon followed the Court to Paris. Its migration seemed the signal for a vigorous application of the pickaxe to the old feudal system by this hitherto "moderate" body. The chief bulwark attacked was the property and independent organisation of the Church. Prior to this, however, the Assembly had reconstituted the Map of France, by abolishing the old division into provinces, substituting for it the present one into departments. The provinces had in the middle ages formed *de facto* independent states. The division into departments placed the whole realm under one central administration, and included the entire reorganisation of the judicial system. There were eighty-three departments formed, which were divided into districts, and these into cantons. The department had its administrative council and executive directory, as had also the district; the canton was merely an electoral sub-division The commune, or township, was confided to a general council and a municipality, which were subordinated to the departmental council. All elections were indirect, and the whole scheme in this respect seemed carefully arranged to exclude, as far as possible, the working classes and peasantry from any effective voice in legislation.

The nationalisation of the Church lands and property

generally was precipitated by the old trouble, the exhausted state of the treasury. Necker had devised every conceivable plan for raising the wind and failed, when the last-named project was suggested as a means of at least temporarily satisfying the exigencies of the situation. It would be tiresome, in a sketch like the present, to describe in detail the stages by which the Assembly arrived at the final result. The issue of its deliberations, to wit, the decree expropriating the Church, was carried on the 2nd of December, and thenceforth the churchmen as a body became the determined enemies of the new *regime*. At first the clergy seemed more inclined than the *noblesse* to compromise matters, in the hope of retaining their wealth, but now that the die was cast they were implacable. The difficulties attending the sale of the ecclesiastical property, however, were too great to admit of its realisation in time for the pressing needs of the exchequer, hence the issue of *assignats*, or notes having a forced currency, based on the value of the expropriated lands. This, which meant the adoption of a system of paper money on a vast scale, staved off the imminent financial ruin.

All these measures were very interesting, and showed a laudable activity on the part of the body politic ; but they did not affect the crowds to be seen daily at the bakers' shops, ever and anon breaking out into tumult. The working-classes of Paris had gone to Versailles demanding simply bread, and Lafayette had given them— the royal family ! Any further grumbling was obviously to be suppressed with drastic measures. Accordingly martial law was proclaimed, and the municipality empowered to forcibly disperse any assembly of people having once summoned them to retire. Lafayette was there to put this regulation into effect at the first opportunity. But it did not come yet.

The clubs were now beginning to play a leading part in influencing public opinion. The principal were those of the Jacobins and the Cordeliers. A third club was instituted subsequently by Lafayette, called the Feuillants, and representing " constitutional " principles. The Jacobins' club, destined hereafter to become the great unofficial expression of the Revolution, counted but few prominent adherents in the Assembly, though Barnave and the Lameths were among its members, and it was occasionally patronised by several of the Constitution-makers, including Mirabeau himself. One cadaverous figure, also a deputy, was always at the Jacobins', his dress and speeches alike carefully prepared—by name Maximilian Robespierre, by profession advocate, a native of Arras.

The club of the Cordeliers was composed of an advanced section of the Jacobins. Among its constant attendants might have been seen the stalwart yeoman Danton, and the short, thick-set, sharp-featured journalist Marat. But neither the clubs nor their rising orators at this time exercised more than an indirect influence on the course of events, though they energetically debated every question as it arose.

Meanwhile, in spite of occasional disturbances, and panics as to the King plotting his flight, affairs moved along with comparative smoothness towards the completion of the constitution, the consummation of the middle-class political order.

Preparations for celebrating the anniversary of the fall of the Bastille with due solemnity went on apace. A national confederation was to be held in the Champ de Mars on this occasion in honour of the constitution. The " advanced " members of the *noblesse*, not to be behind in " patriotism," proposed in view of the national fête the abolition of titles, armorial bearings, and the feudal insignia generally. The proposition was enthusiastically carried by the Assembly. Its result was naturally to rouse the keenest indignation among the nobles outside and to give further edge to the organised movement of aristocratic emigration.

On the 14th of July, 1790, the population of Paris, notwithstanding bad weather, were to be seen streaming from all sides in holiday attire, amide a blaze of tricolour—banners, hangings, cockades—to the Champ de Mars, where a gigantic altar had been erected in the centre of a vast artificial amphitheatre. The Royal Family, the Assembly and the municipality were grouped around this altar, before which the then popular Bishop of Autun, Talleyrand (subsequently the famous diplomatist and wit) performed mass in high pontifical robes, assisted by four hundred clergy in white surplices. Lafayette first ascended the altar and in the name of the National Guards of the whole realm took the civic oath of fidelity to "the nation, the law, and the King." This was followed by salvos of artillery and prolonged shouts of "Vive la nation!" "Vive le roi!" The president of the Assembly, and all the deputies, the department councils, &c., next took the same oath. But the grand item of the day's programme was reached when Louis XVI. himself rose to swear, as King of France, to maintain the constitution decreed by the Assembly. This part of the performance terminated, as usual on great occasions, with the appearance of the Queen holding the Dauphin up aloft to the homage and admiration of the assembled multitude, who responded in one long and continuous acclamation. Chants of thanksgiving and exultant jubilation generally closed the day's proceedings.

Such was the inauguration of the first French Constitution! But despite the new and glorious liberty, crowds of hungry Parisians continued to be daily turned away from the bakers' shops.

CHAPTER VII.

A "CONSTITUTION" ON ITS BEAM ENDS.

ALL state functionaries, military, civil and ecclesiastical, were now compelled to take the oath of allegiance to the new order of things. This led to a revolt on the part of the majority of the nobles and ecclesiastics, whose indignation was already roused to boiling point by the loss respectively of their privileges and revenues. Numbers of aristocratic officers left the army and the country to join their brethren across the frontier. Others, such as Bouillé, gave in with the view of gaining over the army for the counter-Revolution. The regular army at this time was almost entirely officered by aristocrats, a fact which gave rise to numerous revolts. A mutiny of three regiments, at Nancy, was only quelled after much bloodshed by Bouillé.

Most of the clergy refused either to take the oath of allegiance or to leave their benefices except by force, being backed up in this by the enormous majority of the bishops with the Pope at their head. The new constitution, in subordinating the ecclesiastical to the civil power, was declared to involve an encroachment on ecclesiastical privilege, the Pope refusing to consecrate bishops in place of those deposed for non-compliance, and proclaiming the creation of all ecclesiastics nominated according to civil forms to be null and void. The ejection of non-conforming priests continued, notwithstanding, their successors being instituted by the bishops of Autun and Lida, who had unreservedly accepted the constitution. The opposite party retaliated by excommunicating all who acknowledged the "intruders," as they termed them. Thus began civil war between the Revolution and the Church. The clergy themselves prepared the soil of the popular mind for the reception and germination of the teachings of the pre-revolutionary writers, which, until now, had been chiefly confined to the leisured and cultivated classes, by forcing it to the logical dilemma of friendship with the "Revolution" and enmity with Christianity, or friendship with Christianity and enmity with the "Revolution."

As regards the "emigrant" aristocrats, their object was to foment the hatred of the foreign Powers against the Revolution and to cement a coalition to effect its forcible overthrow by the invasion of the country. For well-nigh three years these intrigues with the "foreigner" were going on with the connivance of the Court, until the fall of the monarchy precipitated "war to the knife" with the powers in the shape of the campaign known as the "Revolutionary War." To understand the position of affairs it is necessary to remember that since the collapse of feudalism as a living political order, with its quarrels between the titular King and his more or less nominally vassal barons, power had been concentrated more and more in royal hands, while nationalities had become definitely fixed. The result was that the mainly internal politics of the feudal period had from the sixteenth century onwards been giving place to external politics, in which the sovereigns of Europe, having ceased to fear the rivalry of nobles within their jurisdiction, discovered causes of quarrel with their brother sovereigns without—usually in the hope of gaining territory. The French Revolution marks the opening, for the Continent, at least, of the modern period of the struggle of sovereigns, not with their nobles or with each other, but with peoples, that is, with the middle-class backed by the proletariat. This struggle began in England more than a hundred years earlier than on the Continent, but practically subsided again with the Revolution of 1689.

The three principal European Powers were at this time England, France, and Austria. Prussia was a still rising monarchy, and the great Muscovite empire loomed in the background. The petty German princelets might be reckoned upon to side with one or other of the greater powers according to circumstances.

The death of Mirabeau, in April, 1791, having removed all hope of making a successful stroke on behalf of Royalism in the Assembly, the Court turned its attention to military plotting with increased energy. On the other hand, the King felt some misgivings at being re-established exclusively by the aid of foreign bayonets, more especially as his cousin, the Comte d'Artois, was the leader in the movement, and if it were successful might possibly obtain more than his due share of influence in the resuscitated realm. These considerations led the Court to turn a favourable ear to General Bouillé, whose plan was to conquer the Revolution by means of the troops already at hand in the service of the King. The army was to be moved to the frontier, the royal family were then to escape into its midst, after which war was to be declared against the Assembly, and the troops to march on the capital. This arrangement was effected up to the point of the King's flight on the 21st of June, 1791, almost without a hitch. Bouillé, with his army, was ready and waiting for the royal party, when poor Louis was accidentally recognised at Varennes, and brought back a prisoner to Paris. The indignation of the populace knew no bounds. The royal cortege re-entered Paris in the midst of sullen and angry crowds. For the first time serious talk of a Republic was heard. Barnave and the Lameths became the leaders of the Constitutional party in the Assembly, now that Mirabeau was dead. But it was with difficulty that the Constitutionalists could reinstate the King after his voluntary and treacherous abdication. They were only successful in their efforts after having thrown as a sop to Cerberus the condition that if he retracted his oath to the Constitution, if he should place himself at the head of an army, or permit others to do so, he should lose his inviolability and be considered and treated as an ordinary citizen.

But opinion outside of the Assembly was far from satisfied. The leaders of the Jacobin Club (which was now the centre of a federation of similar clubs throughout the country), among whom were confounded in one cause, Brissot, Pétion, Robespierre, Danton, Marat, &c., men of the advanced middle-class and men of the people, combined to rouse the nation against this decree, insisting on the abdication of Louis, and denying the competency of the Assembly. They drew up a petition in which they appealed from the Assembly to the sovereignty of the people. This petition was taken to the Champ de Mars and laid upon the "altar of the country." Thousands came to sign it; the assemblage being dispersed by Lafayette, returned subsequently in greater numbers than before. Next time the commandant of the National Guard came accompanied by Bailly the mayor. The red flag, the then symbol of martial law, was unfurled, the summons to disperse proclaimed, after which Lafayette gave the order to fire. A murderous charge followed, in which hundreds were killed and wounded. But notwithstanding that the Republicans were cowed for the time being, the Court sycophant, and his accomplices in the work of the Constitution, were well-nigh played out, though the old farce had first to be gone through. The King once more accepted the Constitution, and the terms of his re-instatement in possession of his functions in addition, made a touching and heart-stirring speech to the Assembly, was received with effusive demonstrations of affection, &c. The Constituent Assembly, which had been made up of the abortive States-General, then formally proclaimed itself dissolved, its members magnanimously renouncing the right of re-election.

CHAPTER VIII.

THE LEGISLATIVE ASSEMBLY.

THE new Legislative Assembly, as it was called, to distinguish it from the first or Constituent Assembly, commenced its sittings on the 1st of October, 1791. Without, the coalition of Europe against the Revolution was complete. England was united with Prussia and Austria, while the petty German States eagerly joined in this conspiracy to suppress the French nation. The famous treaty of Pilnitz was the expression of the determination and temper of the powers great and small.

Within, the fabric of the constitutional monarchy was standing, indeed ; but, as Carlyle expresses it, like an inverted pyramid, which may topple over any moment. Friction began at once between the King and Assembly on questions of reciprocal etiquette, but the speech from the throne was well received.

The dominant party in this Assembly was that of the Girondists, or party of compromise, of which more anon, the buffer, so to speak, between the Constitutionalists proper, now in the minority, and the popular and avowedly Republican party, whose leaders in the clubs, Robespierre, Danton, Marat, &c., were gaining in influence every day.

Almost the first act of the New Assembly was the issue of a decree ordering the emigrants to return on penalty of death and confiscation of goods. This order the King peremptorily vetoed. The same fate befell another order of the Assembly, by which refractory priests should lose their pay and be placed under surveillance. His action in these matters, in view of the imminent invasion of the foreign powers and the peasant revolt in the Vendeé in favour of Royalism (which was led by the clergy), were fatal to him, and to the Constitutionalists who supported him.

The Constitutional Ministry fell, and a Girondin Ministry was appointed in its place, with Roland, one of the principal Girondin leaders and the husband of the celebrated Madame Roland, as Minister of the Interior, and Dumouriez as Minister of Foreign Affairs.

The first act of the new Ministry was to take the bull by the horns, and to declare war with Austria, a measure popular on various sides, for different reasons, and approved of by the Court in the hope of the defeat of the French forces and the invasion of the country. This declaration of war was made on the 20th of April, 1792. Three columns proceeded to the frontier, but the projected action on the offensive was a fiasco—a panic seizing the troops on the approach of the enemy.

Thenceforward, the French assumed the defensive. Such was the beginning of the Revolutionary War. The news of the disaster led to bitter recriminations, on the part of the popular party, against the Girondins. The Girondins in their turn threw the blame on the Constitutionalists, and their commanders, Lafayette, Dillon, &c., while the generals themselves threw it on Dumouriez. The Jacobins openly accused the Moderate parties of treachery and connivance with the Government. Suspicion and distrust were universal. It was now that Marat issued his memorable placards calling for the heads of traitors. Meanwhile, to appease the people, the Ministry instituted a permanent camp of 20,000 men in the neighbourhood of Paris, in spite of the vehement opposition of the Constitutionalists, and agreed to the introduction into the new National Guard of promiscuously selected companies armed with pikes—the weapons which had played such a prominent part at an earlier stage of the Revolution. The Assembly, which declared itself sitting in

c

permanence, added to these resolutions one ordering the abolition of the King's bodyguard. This last decree Louis at once refused to ratify, and on being remonstrated with by Roland, dismissed all the Girondin ministers, and appointed obscure members of the Constitutionalist party in their stead. At the same time he sent a secret messenger to negotiate with the foreign coalition—for his " deliverance."

The Girondins finding themselves thus left out in the cold, joined the Jacobins, who were now the advanced guard of the Revolution, and whose organisation was rapidly becoming a rival to the Assembly, and by this means were able to pose as martyrs in the cause of liberty. The only hope of the party actually in power, —*i.e.*, the now discredited Constitutionalists—lay in Lafayette's army. Lafayette, seeing the situation, played out his last card, and published a manifesto openly defying and threatening the Jacobins. The Jacobins' reply to this was the insurrection of the 20th June, 1792, when a concourse numbering some 8,000 people left the Faubourg St. Antoine for the hall of the Assembly. The orator who represented the crowd spoke in menacing terms, saying that the people were ready to employ all their powers in resistance to oppression. He proceeded to state that grave complaint was found with the conduct of the war, into which the people demanded an immediate investigation, but the heaviest grievance of all was the dismissal of the patriot Ministers. The Assembly replied that the memorial of the people should be taken into consideration, and meanwhile, as usual in such cases, exhorted them to "respect the law." By this time the multitude numbered some 30,000 men, women, and children, including many National Guards, with a liberal sprinkling of pikes, flags, and revolutionary emblems among them. This motley concourse poured into the sacred precincts of the Assembly, singing "Ça Ira," and shouting, "Long live the people!" "Long live the *sansculottes!*" On leaving the Assembly the cry was, "To the Palace of the Tuileries," where the crowd swept through the open gates into the apartments and corridors, and were proceeding to demolish the doors with blows when Louis himself appeared, accompanied by only a few attendants. The multitude still pressing in, he took his station in the recess of a window. There he remained seated on a chair, placed on a table, and protected from the pressure of the crowd by a cordon of National Guards. To the cries of the people for his sanction to the decrees, he replied—as the Royalist historians assure us with intense dignity—"This is neither the manner for it to be demanded of me, nor the moment to obtain it." The result of his refusal might have been awkward for him had he not had the presence of mind to take advantage of an incident which occurred just at the moment. A red Phrygian cap, the symbol of the People and of Liberty, was presented by one of the crowd on the point of a pike. This he took and placed on his head, after which he drank off a tankard of wine also offered to him, an act which was greeted with tumultuous applause. At last Pétion, the mayor, arrived with several prominent Girondist deputies, and quietly dispersed the gathering.

Thus the silly Parisian populace were once again cajoled out of their demands by a senseless piece of buffoonery. But it was the last time. The Constitutionalists were enraged at the outrage offered to the person of the King and to the Law. Lafayette left the army, and suddenly appeared at the bar of the Assembly demanding the impeachment of the instigators of the movement of the 20th July, and the suppression of the popular clubs. But the Jacobins had by this time got the upper hand, and could defy the champion of middle-class law-and-order. Lafayette narrowly escaped arrest for deserting his army, and had ignominiously to slink back. The whole force of the populace was with the Girondins and the Jacobins. Things were fast hurrying to a crisis.

CHAPTER IX.

THE TENTH OF AUGUST.

SHORTLY after the event last described the Assembly felt itself compelled, in face of the open connivance of the Court with the enemy, to solemnly declare the country in danger. All citizens capable of bearing arms were called upon to enroll themselves in the National Guard, which was placed on a footing of active service.

On the 14th of July, the Bastille anniversary, the Mayor Pétion was the hero of the day—"Pétion or death!" being the popular watchword. All battalions of the National Guard showing signs of attachment to Constitutionalism instantly became objects of popular resentment. The hatred of the Constitutionalists was daily growing. At length the popular party obtained the disbandment of the companies of Grenadiers and Chasseurs, the main support of the official middle-class in the National Guard, together with the closing of the Feuillants' Club, the rendezvous of the Constitutionalist party.

Events further helped on the popular cause. On the 25th of July, the Duke of Brunswick published his manifesto in the name of the Emperor and the King of Prussia, in which he declared that the allied sovereigns had taken up arms to put an end to anarchy in France; threatening all the towns which dared to resist with total destruction, the members of the Assembly itself with the rigours of martial law, &c. The active coalition which was at this time confined to Prussia, Austria, the German princedoms, and the principality of Turin, had

formed the plan of marching concentrically upon Paris
from three different points, the Moselle, the Rhine and
the Netherlands.

It was on the day of the movement of the Rhenish
division from Coblentz, under the command of the Duke
of Brunswick, that this famous manifesto was issued.
The following day, July 26th, a contingent of six hundred Marseillais, sent for by the Girondist Barbaroux,
who was a native of Marseilles, entered Paris ostensibly on
their way to the camp at Soissons, a contingent rendered
immortal by the hymn they sang as they marched along;
the well-known strains:

> " Allons, enfants de la Patrie,
> Le jour de gloire est arrivé,"

having been heard for the first time in the streets of
Paris on that occasion. The advent of the Marseillais,
though it did not, as was anticipated, result in an
immediate outbreak, did, nevertheless, stir Paris to its
foundations. The sections, or wards, into which the city
was divided, became daily more importunate in demanding the dethronement of the King. A petition to this
effect was drawn up by the municipality and the sections
and presented to the Assembly by Pétion on the 3rd of
August. The impeachment of Lafayette was next demanded on the 8th, but after a warm discussion was
rejected by a considerable majority. This acquittal of
Lafayette, now regarded by the people as the personifica-
tion of treachery and reaction, destroyed the last vestige
of popular confidence in the Assembly. The following
day one of the sections sent to notify to the legislature
that if the decree of dethronement were not voted before
nightfall the *tocsin* (or alarm bell) should be sounded, the
générale (or rallying drum) beaten, and open insurrection
proclaimed, a determination which was transmitted to
the forty-eight sections of the city, and approved with

only one dissentient. It was not voted, and the same evening the Jacobins proceeded in a body to the Faubourg St. Antoine, and there organised the attack on the Tuileries which it was decided should take place the next day.

Measures pregnant with import for the future course of the Revolution were determined at this meeting; among others the dismissal of the Girondist mayor, Pétion, who had already begun to inspire deep distrust, the annulment of the Departmental Assemblies, and replacement of the old municipal council by a Revolutionary Commune.

At midnight the tocsin pealed, the générale beat, the sections assembled, and the newly-nominated Commune took possession of the Hotel de Ville. On the other side the "loyal" battalions of the National Guard were marched to the palace, which was now filled with hired Swiss Guards and *Chevaliers de Cour*, and the Assembly hastily called together. On hearing that Pétion was detained at the Tuileries the moribund legislature at once ordered his release and restored him to his functions. But he no sooner entered the Hotel de Ville than he was placed under a guard of three hundred men by order of the new Commune. Poor Pétion! between two fires! The Commune then sent for the commander of the National Guard, Mandat, who was at the Tuileries with the royal battalions aforesaid. Mandat, not knowing of the creation of the new Commune, incautiously obeyed the summons, but turned pale on discovering new faces where he had expected to find the old municipal councillors. He was accused of having authorised the troops to defend the palace against the sovereign people, was ordered to the prison of the Abbaye, but was assassinated on the steps of the Hotel de Ville as he was being conveyed thither. Santerre was then nominated commander-in-chief in his stead.

Meanwhile not a few "Nationals" at the palace, in spite of their loyalty to the "Constitution," winced at finding themselves in the same galley with aristocrat adventurers—avowed enemies of the Revolution in any form or shape—and with mercenary foreign soldiers. Their leader gone, a division broke out, as Louis found when he came to review them, for while the cry, "Vive le roi!" was responded to by some, "Vive la nation!" was reponded to by more. But what was most ominous was the arrival of two fresh battalions armed with pikes as well as guns, who after jeeringly greeting the king with shouts of "Vive la nation!" "Down with the veto!" "Down with the traitor!" took up a position at the Pont Royal and pointed their cannon straight at the palace. It was evident the loyalty of these battalions was more than a doubtful quantity. It was now early morning, and the insurgents were advancing in columns of various strength from different points. The Procurator-Syndic, Roederer, met them as they were converging upon the palace, and suggested their sending a deputation to the king. This was peremptorily refused. He then addressed himself to the National Guard, reading out the articles which enjoined them to suppress revolt. But the response was so feeble that the procurator fled in all haste back to the Tuileries to urge the royal family to leave its quarters and place itself in the midst of the Assembly out of harm's reach. Marie Antoinette rejected the advice in right melodramatic style, talked very "tall" about being "nailed to the walls of the palace," and presented a pistol to Louis with the words, "Now, sire, is the moment to show your courage." The procurator evidently thought mock heroics ill-timed, and sternly remonstrated. Louis himself seemed to share this opinion, or at least was not prepared to "show" his "courage" just then, and moved to go to the Assembly. Marie Antoinette followed with the royal youth, and thus what bid fair to be a dramatic "situation" came to an ignominious ending.

Meanwhile the insurgents surrounded the palace, the defence of which was left to the Swiss Guard, who, though they fought with a valour worthy of a better cause, were ultimately overwhelmed by numbers and exterminated. The palace taken, shouts of victory resounded from far and near. The Assembly trembled, expecting every minute the hall to be forced. In vain it issued a proclamation conjuring the people to respect magistrates, law and justice. At length the new Commune presented itself, claiming the recognition of its powers, the dethronement of the king, and the convocation of a National Convention by universal suffrage. Deputation after deputation followed with the same prayer, or rather with the same peremptory order. The Assembly, overawed, on the motion of the Girondist Vergniaud, passed a resolution in pursuance of the demands, that is, suspending the King, dismissing the Constitutionalist Ministers, and ordering the convocation of a National Convention.

The person of Louis, after remaining three days in charge of the Assembly, was handed over to the Commune, by whose order he was conveyed as a State prisoner to the Temple. Thus ended the 10th of August, 1792. The critical struggle is henceforth not, as heretofore, between the middle-class and the nobles or the King, but between the middle-class and the proletariat.

CHAPTER X.

THE FIRST PARIS COMMUNE AND THE SEPTEMBER MASSACRES.

WITH the 10th of August and the overthrow of the Monarchy, the first part of the French Revolution may be considered as complete. The middle-class insurrection proper had done its work. The importance of that work from certain points of view can hardly be over-rated. In a word, it had abolished, not, indeed, feudalism in its true sense—for that had long since ceased to exist—but the corrupt remains of feudalism and the monarchical despotism it left behind it. The beginning of '89 found France cut up into provinces, each in many respects an independent State, possessing separate customs, separate laws, and in some cases a separate jurisdiction. The end of '89 even, and still more '92, found it, for good or evil, a united nationality. The power of the clergy and noblesse was completely broken. Judicial torture and breaking on the wheel were absolutely done away with. Madame Roland has described the dying cries of the victims of "justice," who, after having been mangled by the latter hideous engine, were left exposed on the market-place, "so long as it shall please God to prolong their lives." All this, then, was abolished, and in addition the "goods" of the clergy and of the "emigrant" nobility were declared confiscated. The interesting point as yet unsolved was, who should get this precious heritage, the "nationalised" lands, houses, and moveable possessions of the recalcitrant first and second estates? To avoid interrupting the narrative we shall devote a chapter to the elucidation of this point later on.

We come now to what we may term the great tidal wave of the Revolution. For the time being it swept all before it, but it receded as quickly as it came. The period of the ascendancy of the proletariat lasted from the 10th of August, 1792, to the 27th of July, 1794, thus in all nearly two years. The political revolution suddenly became transformed into a revolution one of whose objects at least was greater social and economical, as distinguished from political, equality, and as suddenly ceased to be so. The course of the progress and retrogression of this movement we shall trace in the following chapters.

The new revolutionary municipality, or Commune of Paris, was now for the time being the most powerful executive body in all France. It dictated the action even of the Assembly. The establishment of an extraordinary tribunal had been proposed. The Assembly hesitated to agree to it, whereupon it received a message from the Commune that if such a tribunal were not forthwith constituted, an insurrection should be organised the following night which should overwhelm the elect of France. The Assembly yielded under the pressure, and a Court was formed which condemned a few persons, but was soon after abolished by the Commune as inadequate. At the head of the latter body were Marat, Panis, Collot-d'Herbois, Billaud-Varennes, Tallien, &c., but the most prominent man of all was for the moment Danton, who was untiring in organising the "sections" (as the different wards of the city were called), and who, from having been the chief agent in the events of the 10th, had acquired almost the position of dictator.

Meanwhile the invading army of the Prussians had crossed the frontier, while the French frontier troops at Sedan, deserted by Lafayette, were disorganised, and

without a commander. On the 24th of August, the
citadel of Longwy capitulated, and by the 30th the
enemy were bombarding the town of Verdun. In a few
days the road to Paris would lie open before them.
Consternation prevailed in the capital at the news. In a
conference between the Ministry and the recently
formed Committee of General Defence, Danton boldly
urged, as against a policy of waiting or of open attack,
that one of terrorism should be adopted, to first intimidate
the reactionary population of the city, and through
them that of the whole country. "The 10th of August,"
said he, "has divided France into two parties. The
latter, which it is useless to dissemble constitutes the
minority in the State, is the only one on which you can
depend when it comes to the combat." The timid and
irresolute Ministry hesitated; Danton betook himself
to the Commune. His project was accepted. The
minority had indeed to fight the majority. Domiciliary
visits were made during the night, and so large a number
of suspected persons arrested, that the prisons were
filled to overflowing. A vast number of citizens were en-
rolled on the Champ de Mars, and dispatched to the
frontier on the 1st of September. About two o'clock the
next day, Sunday, the great bell or *tocsin* was sounded,
the call-drum or *générale* was beaten along the thoroughfares, the famous September massacres were at hand.
Danton, in presenting himself before the Assembly to
detail the measures that had been taken (without its
consent) for the safety of the country, gave utterance to
his celebrated *mot* :—" *Il faut de l'audace, de l'audace, et
toujours de l'audace*" (we must have boldness, boldness,
and always boldness).

The previous night all the gates of the city had
been closed by order of the municipality, so that none
could leave or enter; to the clanging of the *tocsin* and
the roll of the *générale*, was now added the firing
of alarm cannon. Herewith began the summary

executions, as they would have been called had they
been done in the interests of "established order" by
men in uniform, or massacres, as they have been termed
since they were effected in the interests of revolution by
men in *bonnet rouge* and Carmagnole costume. The
matter originated with the destruction of thirty priests
who were being conducted to the Abbaye. The prisons,
about seven in number, were then visited in succession
by a band of some three hundred men. Entrance was
demanded by an improvised court, which, once inside,
with the prison-registers open before them, began to adju-
dicate. The prisoners were severally called by name,
their cases decided in a few minutes, after which they
were successively removed nominally to another prison,
or to be released. No sooner, however, had they reached
the outer gate than they were met by a forest of pikes
and sabres. Those that were deemed innocent of
treasonable practices, and were "enlarged" with the cry
of "*Vive la nation!*" (Long live the nation!), were received with embracings and acclamation, but woe betide
those who were conducted to the entrance in silence.
Upon them the pikes and sabres at once fell, in some
cases veritably hewing them in pieces. The Princesse
de Lamballe, the friend and maid-of-honour to Marie
Antoinette, had just gone to bed when the crowd arrived
at the Abbaye where she was imprisoned. On being
informed she was about to be removed, she wanted to
arrange her dress, she said; at which the bystanders
hinted that from the distance she would have to go, it
was scarcely worth while to waste much time on the
toilette. Arrived at the gate, her head was struck off,
and her body stripped and disembowelled. A Sansculotte
subsequently boasted of having cooked and eaten one of
the breasts of the princess. Carlyle goes into an ecstatic
frenzy over Mdlle. de Lamballe. "She was beautiful, she
was good," he exclaims (vol. iii., chap. 4), in a style sugges-
tive of an Irish wake. "Oh! worthy of worship, thou king-

descended, god-descended," &c. He pathetically talks
about her "fair hind-head," meaning to imply, I suppose,
that she had a long, thin neck. But inasmuch as there
is no physiological reason for supposing that a long, thin
neck involves greater suffering to the possessor in the
process of decapitation than a short, thick one, the point
of the remark is not obvious. Be this as it may, the
princess's head, with others, was paraded on a pike
through the streets and under the windows of the
"Temple," where the queen was confined. These summary
executions or massacres (according as we choose to call
them) outside the prisons, continued at intervals from
the Sunday afternoon to the Thursday evening. Probably about 1,200 persons in all perished. All contemporary writers agree in depicting the graphic horror
of the scene as the blood-stained crowd swept along the
streets from prison to prison.

There is no doubt that the principal actors in these
events were either under the orders, or were at least in
communication with the Commune, but the precise nature
of the connection has not been, and possibly now never
will be, known. That those concerned were no mere
wanton or mercenary ruffians, but fanatics, possessed by
a frenzy of despair, is amply proved by several incidents
which are admitted even by Royalist writers. Their
enthusiasm at the discovery of a "patriot" in one whom
they believed to have been a "plotter," as in the case of
M. de Sombreuil, and their refusal of money from such,
their evident desire to avoid by any accident the death
of an innocent person, show the executioners to have
been, at least, genuinely disinterested. There has never
in all history been more excuse for the shedding of
blood than there was in Paris, at the beginning of
September, 1792. Foreign troops were marching on the
capital to destroy the Revolution, and all favourable to
it. The city itself was honeycombed with Royalist
plotters, who almost openly expressed their joy at the

prospect of an approaching restoration, and the exter-
mination of the popular leaders. The so-called massacres
were strictly a measure of self-defence, and as such were
justified by the result, which was, in a word, to strike
terror into the reaction, and to stimulate the Revolution
throughout France ; and yet there are bourgeois who
pretend to view this strictly defensive act of a populace
driven to desperation, with shuddering horror, while
regarding as "necessary," or at most midly disapproving
the wanton and cold-blooded massacres of the Versailles
soldiers after the Commune of 1871. Such, verily, is
class blindness! As in all great crisis in history, so in
the French Revolution, an active minority had to fight
and terrorise the stolid mass of reaction and indifference
which, alas! is always in the majority.

CHAPTER XI.

THE NATIONAL CONVENTION.

WHILE these events were going on in Paris, Dumouriez, the successor of Lafayette as commander-in-chief of the French army, was in the east organising the resistance to the invasion. Verdun was taken by the Prussians almost without resistance. But the new commander, who, whatever else he may have been, was a man of military genius, saw at a glance the strategical situation, and, in opposition to the council of war, decided to lose no time in occupying the passes of the mountainous district of the Argonne. He circumvented the enemy by forced marches, and they soon found the road to Paris barred by precipitous rocks and well-guarded passes. The Prussians, notwithstanding, forced one of the more feebly defended of the positions, and were on the point of surrounding the French army when Dumouriez, by a dexterous retreat, succeeded in evading them till the arrival of his reinforcements. Meanwhile, the weather helped the defenders. Heavy rains converted the bad roads into rivers of mud knee deep, and it was not until the 20th of the month that the main body of the invaders reached the heights of Valmy, where General Kellerman was in command, and which they attempted to storm. The result decided the fate of the invasion. The Prussians and Austrians were completely defeated to the cry of "Vive la nation!" and retired in disorder. Up to this time the fortunes of war had been unremittingly adverse to the French. But the turning point had come. Henceforward the revolutionary army, which from this moment assumed the offensive, went forth for some time conquering and to conquer. The present sketch not being a history of the revolutionary war, but of the Revolution itself, I shall in future only allude to the military situation in so far as it affects the course of internal affairs.

The moribund Legislative Assembly lingered on during the election of the Convention—the first political body chosen by direct, universal and equal suffrage—which did not open its deliberations till the 21st of the month. After the usual preliminaries it formally abolished Royalty, and proclaimed the Republic. Its next measure was to declare the new era to date from the current year as the first year of the French Republic. These measures were carried by acclamation. But the Convention almost immediately became the prey of internal dissention. This most remarkable of legislative bodies embraced every shade of opinion and almost all the men of any prominence in public life. Robespierre, Danton, Marat, Desmoulins, David, Roland, Barbaroux, Siéyes, Barrére, &c., were all now to the fore, with many others, such as Tallien, Collot d'Herbois, Billaud Varennes, Barras, &c., hitherto less known to fame, but shortly to come into unmistakable prominence. One feature of the Convention is especially remarkable. It embodied the first conscious recognition of the principle of Internationalism. The German atheist, internationalist and humanitarian, Anacharsis Clootz, and the English freethinker and republican Thomas Paine, were among its members. Priestly, of Birmingham, the great chemist, had also been elected, but declined to sit. In order at once to accentuate the international conception of the Revolution and to create a diversion in the rear of the invading armies, the Convention issued a manifesto on Nov. 19 inviting all peoples to rise against their oppressors and assuring them of the sympathy and, when possible, of the active support of the French Republic.

The two great parties in the Convention were the

Girdondists and the Mountainists. The Girondists were
the party of orderly progress, sweetness, and light, the
men who dreaded all violent, *i.e.*, energetic measures.
Such men, however well-intentioned they may be, and
even apart from their ultimate objects, must always in
the long run become the tools of reaction from their
timidity and hesitancy. The Girondists desired a
doctrinaire Republic, led by the professional middle-
classes, the lawyers and *littérateurs*. Their main strength
lay in the provinces, the name being derived from the
department of the Gironde, whence some of their chief
men came. Among the leaders of the Girondist party
may be mentioned Condorcet, Roland, Louvet, Rebecqé,
Pétion, Barbaroux, Vergniaud, and Brissot. Some of
them had been, in spite of their generally mild attitude,
active in preparing the 10th of August. It was, as we
have seen, Barbaroux who sent to his native town for
the Marseillais, and directed this remarkable body of men
on the day of the insurrection.

The other leading party in the Convention were the
Mountainists, as they were termed, because they sat on
the benches at the top of the left, comprising the leaders
of Paris and largely identical in policy with the
Commune, many of whose members sat in both the
municipal and the legislative bodies. Robespierre,
Danton, Marat, all the Parisian members, that is, the
most advanced revolutionary leaders, belonged to the
" Mountain," which had its strength in the 48 " sections,"
and in the faubourgs, or outlying suburbs, in which the
populace of Paris found voice. The Mountainists advocated uncompromising revolutionary principles (besides
aiming to some extent at economic equality), a vigorous
policy and a strong centralisation in opposition to the
Girondists, who favoured strictly middle-class Republican-
ism, a timid and vacillating policy, and federalisation, or
local autonomy. The struggle between the Mountain and
Gironde was in part a struggle for supremacy between

Paris and the departments. Besides the Mountainists and Girondists proper—*i.e.*, those who represented any definite principles at all, who both together constituted a minority in the Convention, notwithstanding that they dictated its character and policy—there was the actual majority which was called the *Plain*, its members being sometimes designated, in ridicule, "frogs of the marsh." Like most majorities, the Plain was an inchoate mass of floating indifferentism and muddle-headedness, with more or less reactionary instincts, which naturally inclined it to the side of the Girondists as the "moderate" party, but whose first concern being self-preservation, was open to outside pressure from the armed "sections" of Paris and the faubourgs, as we shall presently see. These "men of the plain," or "frogs of the marsh," included many persons of ability, who subsequently came to the front under the Directorate, after all danger of popular insurrection was at an end.

War was declared within the Convention, before many days were over, by the Gironde, on the ostensible pretext of the September massacres, which they accused the partisans of the Mountain of having instigated. The individuals attacked were Robespierre and Marat. It was the turn of Robespierre first. He was accused of aspiring to the dictatorship, and the whole force of Girondist eloquence was brought to bear upon the lean and cadaverous ex-advocate of Arras, though without result. No definite charges could be formulated against him. It is significant, nevertheless, that before Robespierre had attained any supreme prominence he should have excited feelings of such keen personal animosity. As a matter of fact, Danton had had far more directly to do with the so-called massacres than Robespierre. It was Marat's turn next. Marat, whose single-mindedness and absolute self-sacrifice are almost unique in history, had the misfortune to be physically an unattractive personality. He suffered from an unpleasant skin malady, which, as it happens, was *not* syphillis, as many writers have hinted, but seems to have been of the nature of the sheep-disease known as the *scabies.* It was very possibly contracted, and without doubt considerably aggravated, through semi-starvation and the cellar-life he was compelled to lead during the early part of the Revolution. Marat, then, was denounced in the Convention by the Girondins, and when he arose to defend himself he was for a moment basely deserted even by his colleagues of the Mountain. "I have a great many enemies in this Assembly," he said, as he rose to reply to his accusers. "All! All!" shouted the Convention as one man. However, Marat proceeded amidst uproar and howls to exculpate himself, till in the end the simple earnestness of his eloquence prevailed, and he sat down amid a storm of applause. But the Girondists, though discomfited for the time, did not lose sight of their design to destroy Marat. In the midst of these recriminations and internal squabbles, the Mountain succeeded in getting the unity of the Republic decreed, a heavy blow to the Federalist Girondins.

CHAPTER XII.

THE TRIAL AND EXECUTION OF THE KING.

A TRUCE to personal squabbles having been for a moment agreed upon, the Convention was proceeding to discuss the new Constitution when, on the motion of the Mountain, the question of the disposal of the King was declared urgent. The popular resentment against the dethroned monarch had been growing for some time past. Continual addresses from the departments, as well as from the Paris sections, were being received praying for his condemnation. The usual legal questions being raised as to the power of any tribunal to try the sovereign, it was agreed by the Committee appointed to consider the matter, that though Louis had been inviolable as King of France, he was no longer so as the private individual Louis Capet. The Mountain vehemently attacked this view. St. Just, Robespierre, and others declared that these legal quibbles were an insult to the people's sovereignty, that the King had already been judged by virtue of the insurrection, and that nothing remained but his condemnation and execution. Just at this time an iron chest was found behind a panel of the Tuileries, containing damning proofs of Court intrigues with Mirabeau, and with the "emigrant" aristocrats, also indicating that the war with Austria had been urged on with a view to betraying the country and the Revolution. This naturally gave force to the demand for the immediate condemnation of Louis as a "traitor to the French and guilty towards humanity." The agitation was vigorously sustained in the Jacobins' club and in the sections, and the "moderate" party in the Assembly found itself compelled to give heed to the popular outcry, at least up to a certain point. The Convention by a considerable majority decided against the extreme right, who urged the inviolability of the King, and also against those Mountainists who pressed for a condemnation without trial. It was determined to bring the ex-King to the bar of the Convention. The Act declaratory of the Royal crimes was then prepared.

Meanwhile Louis was being strictly guarded in the "Temple," where he had now been confined nearly four months. He had recently been separated from his family, the Commune fearing the concerting of plots of escape. Only one servant was allotted to the whole family. Louis amused himself at this time with reading Hume's History of England, especially the parts relating to Charles I. On the vote of the Convention being declared, Santerre, the commandant of the National Guard, was commissioned to conduct Louis to the bar of the National Assembly. This took place on the 11th of December. The coach passed through drizzling rain, scowling crowds, and through streets filled with troops. Arrived at the hall of the Convention, the Mayor of Paris, Chabot, and the Procureur, Chaumette, who had sat with the King in the vehicle, delivered him over to Santerre, who had been in attendance outside. The latter, laying hold of Louis by the arm, led him to the bar of the Convention. Barrére, the President, after a moment's delay, greeted him with the words, "Louis, the French nation accuses you; you are now about to hear the act of accusation. Louis, you may sit down." There were fifty-seven counts of the indictment relating to acts of despotism, conspiracies, secret intrigues, the flight to Varennes, and what not. On the conclusion of the speech for the prosecution, which lasted three hours, Louis was removed back to his prison. He had demanded legal counsel, so the Convention decided after some discussion to allow his old friend Malesherbes, with two others, Tronchet and Déséze, to undertake the office. It was the latter who delivered the speech on the day of the defence, which consisted partly in the old arguments anent royal inviolability and partly in a statement of Louis's services to the people. "The people," said Déséze, "desired that a disastrous impost should be abolished, and Louis abolished it; the people asked for the abolition of servitudes, and Louis abolished them: they demanded reforms, and he consented to them," &c. &c. The speech concluded with an eloquent peroration calling upon history to judge the decision of the Convention. The cowardly Girondins, although it was well-known they had previously been in favour of the King's life, did not have the courage at this moment to make a definite stand one way or the other. They contented themselves with proposing to declare Louis guilty, but to leave the question of punishment to the primary assemblies of the people. This proposition, which would probably have meant civil war, was vehemently opposed by the Mountain and rejected, and the Convention, after having unanimously voted Louis guilty, resolved on considering the question of punishment. The popular ferment outside the Convention was immense, and sentence of death was loudly demanded. After forty hours, the final vote was taken, and Louis condemned to "death without respite," i.e. within twenty-four hours, by a majority of 26 in an assembly of 721. In vain did the defenders urge the smallness of the majority; the Mountain, which now for the first time dominated the Convention, showed itself inexorable.

On Monday, the 21st of January, 1793, the execution took place. Louis, who had taken leave of his family the previous day, was awakened at five o'clock. Shortly after, Santerre arrived to announce that it was the hour to depart. At the same time the murmur of crowds and the rumbling of cannon were heard outside. The carriage took upwards of an hour to pass through the streets, which were lined with military. At length the Place de la Revolution was reached, and Louis ascended the scaffold. He was beginning to protest his innocence, when on the signal of Santerre his voice was drowned by the beating of drums, the executioner seized him, and in a moment all was over.

The death of Louis was probably necessary for the safety of the Republic at the time, but one cannot help having some pity for one whose worst offences were a certain feebleness and good nature which made him the ready tool of a cruel, unscrupulous, and designing woman. It should be noted, as regards the decree in the Convention, that, unlike the Girondins, plucky Tom Paine, up to the last, manfully voted in the sense in which he had always spoken, viz., for the life of the King, and this at the imminent risk of his own. Notwithstanding this act, a grateful Respectability (which afterwards tried to exalt the feeble Louis into a hero and a martyr) has ever since heaped every vile calumny on poor Paine's memory.

CHAPTER XIII.

ON the evening of the final vote in the Convention on the matter of the King, Lepelletier de St. Fargeaux, a deputy and ex-noble, who had voted with the majority, was assassinated by an ex-royal guard in a café. On the Thursday following he received a public funeral, his remains being interred in the Pantheon of great men. The Convention, Municipality, and all the revolutionary societies followed in a body. This was the last united action of the various parties.

The feud between Mountain and Gironde broke out with renewed fury after the temporary cessation. The quarrel was intensified out of doors by the old but ever-increasing lack of the necessaries of life, especially of bread. The *queues* at the bakers' shops assumed more formidable dimensions, developing into mobs and devastating provision shops. Marat had suggested in his journal that a few of the forestallers who were helping to keep up the price of bread should be hanged at the doors of bakers' shops. The crowds, dressed in carmagnole, or merely ragged, maddened by hunger, danced the more wildly to the well-known strains, " Vive le son du canon." Day and night groups of these revolutionary revellers might be met along the thoroughfares.

Meanwhile " the sound of the cannon " was going on with vigour and to the honour and glory of France. Dumouriez had invaded and conquered the Netherlands, and the Jacobins and other revolutionary bodies had sent missionaries to the newly-annexed provinces. But the powers, great and small, finding themselves and the aristocratic-monarchic order they represented being beaten all along the line, drew closer together and made new levies. England, Spain, Italy, Austria, Prussia, the small German States, hurled new and gigantic armaments into the breach. The Convention answered in its turn by a fresh levy of 300,000 men. But Danton and the Mountain demanded at the same moment that while external enemies were being fought internal enemies should not be neglected. They proposed that a tribunal composed of nine members should judge without jury and without appeal. The tribunal was instituted but the jury added. Dumouriez now sustained some reverses in his invasion of Holland. He was ordered back into Belgium, but this did not satisfy the Mountain and the Jacobins, who had for long looked askance at Dumouriez as a Girondist partisan, and became now more convinced than ever that he was working in the interest of the faction, and that the defeat was due to treachery. The Girondin ministers and generals were the objects of the bitterest resentment. So high did the feeling run that a conspiracy was set on foot to assassinate the leading men of the party in the Convention on the night of the 10th of March. The conspirators, it is alleged, actually set out, but the plan miscarried, owing to its betrayal beforehand to the persons threatened. Vergniaud, the great Girondin orator, denounced the plot next day in the Assembly, and the advanced parties were for a moment checked. But the news of the spread of the aristocratic revolt in the district of the Loire known as La Vendée, quickly enabled them to regain their ascendancy.

The Vendée was a district in which there were no large towns, and consequently hardly any middle-class or proletariat. It was a district inhabited almost exclusively by peasants, priests, and nobles, and consequently altogether out of touch with the objects of the Revolution. The peasantry still venerated their old masters, and hated the new middle-class. The immediate cause of the fresh outbreak, however, was the new levy. In Paris the feeling against "Moderates" and half-hearted friends of the Republic waxed greater than ever. The new Revolutionary Tribunal redoubled its activity. Following upon the bad news from the Vendée came that of further and still more serious reverses in Belgium on the part of Dumouriez, and, what was worse, indisputable evidence of intrigues with the Austrians to reestablish the monarchy in the person of the Duc de Chartres, the young son of Phillipe d'Orleans Egalité (the King's cousin and a member of the Mountain party). This Duc de Chartres, at that time a lieutenant of Dumouriez, became subsequently "Louis Philippe, King of the French." Dumouriez almost immediately after openly proclaimed his intention of marching upon Paris to subdue the Revolution. But he did not succeed any better than Lafayette, his predecessor in the same course. His troops, although attached to him personally, hesitated at treachery to the Republic. The same with the officers. The Convention was energetic; it sent four commissioners, among them the Minister of War, to summon the traitor-general to the bar of the Convention. He not only refused to come, but handed over the commissioners as hostages to the Austrians. After a further fruitless attempt to seduce the army he sought refuge with the Duc de Chartres and a few other officers in the Austrian camp, and from this time history knows him no more. Dumouriez's defection drove the last nail into the coffin of the Girondist power. There is a well-known proverb that those whom the gods would destroy they first make mad. This was certainly exemplified in the present case. For the Girondins had already, before their General Dumouriez's escape had become known, alienated the leading Mountainist who had been in favour of reconciliation between the parties—Danton, to wit—by unsubstantiated insinuations. And now, when Dumouriez's desertion had been for days past a topic of discussion and declamation amongst the Paris sections, they succeeded amid scenes of violent disorder in the Convention in getting a decree of indictment launched against Marat on the ground of the paragraph about the forestallers. The *People's Friend* was accordingly brought before the Revolutionary Tribunal, the Girondists vainly attempting to pack the jury. After a trial lasting two days, he was acquitted amid the acclamations of the audience, and carried in triumph by the populace into the hall of the Convention. Girondism was henceforth plainly a lost cause so far as peaceful and legal action was concerned. Its only hope lay in an insurrection of the departments. This also, as we shall see, was destined to failure. Meanwhile Custine, Dampière, and other generals were sent to reorganise the armies of Dumouriez, but for the next few weeks the main attention of all patriots was directed to one object—the destruction of the Girondist faction.

CHAPTER XIV.

CONCERNING MATTERS ECONOMIC.

AMID all this contention the Mountain, aided by economic pressure, succeeded in forcing through some important
administrative, and two great economic measures. In
addition to the "Revolutionary Tribunal," two powerful
Committees were established which, in the end, practically
assumed all the executive functions of a dictatorial
ministry. These were the "Committee of General Security," consisting of twenty-one members, and the
"Committee of Public Safety," consisting of nine members, the ministers themselves being subject to these Committees. The economic measures referred to were, first, the
Law of *maximum*, by means of which, at a stroke, the
starvation and misery previously existing were allayed.
The law of *maximum* enacted a fixed price for bread-
stuffs, above which it was penal to sell them. To avert
the possibility of the dealers refusing to sell at all, it was
made compulsory upon them to do so. They were, more-
over, obliged to furnish accurate accounts of their stock,
which could, if desirable, be peremptorily "checked" by
the authorities. The law was subsequently extended to
all the necessaries of life. The other economic measure
forced through the Convention by the Jacobins and the
Mountain was a progressive income-tax on an ascending
scale. In addition to these there was a forced loan of a
milliard for war purposes levied on the wealthy classes.
The Girondists and the Plain, of course, shrieked and
kicked at these glaring infringements of the "laws" of
political economy and the rights of property: but the

middle-class factions, though nominally dominant, were not really so, and were hence unable to resist the force of the popular demand for decisive steps in the direction of greater economic equality.

The law of *maximum* and the progressive income-tax are the only two measures of a directly Socialistic tendency which have ever been practically applied, and they were applied with complete success. And yet it is strange that at least the first of these measures, when proposed now-a-days, is viewed by many Socialists with indifference, not to say suspicion. It only shows how, in economics, as in other things, the rags of old superstitions unconsciously survive in us. Those who have triumphed over the old-fashioned *bourgeois* fallacies of the wickedness and inutility of interfering with the sacred laws of political economy by direct legislative interference with the freedom of production, still wince at the notion of direct legislative interference with freedom (so-called) of exchange. An eight-hour law is an excellent thing, but a *maximum*, by which the eight-hour workman is protected from the extortions of monopoly and the power of industrial and commercial capital to raise prices, guarding itself against the effects of competition by "rings" and "corners"—this is a very doubtful thing indeed! In the present day, of course, a law of *maximum* would be of very little use unless supplemented by a law of *minimum*—i.e., a law fixing a minimum wage—and, we may add, parenthetically, the eight hours working day would, in all probability, also prove itself a questionable boon if unaccompanied by both these provisos. But in France at the end of the last century it was not so. The *petite industrie* prevailed everywhere except in the large towns, where the workshop system had obtained a footing, though even there without having by any means entirely supplanted the smaller production. The law of *maximum* alone was therefore sufficient to meet all requirements. Scarcity and want there was still, but it was a scarcity and want due, for the most part, to other than remediable social conditions. Bad harvests, the devastations of foreign invasion and civil war, had reduced France to the lowest ebb. The law of *maximum* saved it. With the two francs a day which was voted at a subsequent period as the allowance of every attendant at the primary assemblies of the sections or wardships, of which there were 44,000 in all France, the problem of the unemployed was solved for the nonce. The number of the unemployed in all trades ministering to the luxuries of the rich may be imagined, and a measure of this kind was absolutely essential.

The net result of the interference by the Convention with the " Laws of Political Economy " is well expressed by Carlyle, where he declares that " there is no period to be met with in which the general 25,000,000 of France suffered less than in this period, which they name reign of terror." Time was as yet not ripe for the great constructive movement of modern Socialism, and hence the merely remedial treatment here explained was all that could even be attempted. The great fact to be noted is that, for the first time in history, the cry for material and social equality as opposed to mere political and legal equality, became definitely articulate. That cry has often enough since been smothered, but has always made itself heard again at short intervals. The party of the Mountain and the Jacobins, the Babœuf conspiracy, the Chartist movement, the days of June, 1848, the Commune of 1871, are all so many stages in the awakening of the Proletariat to the full consciousness of itself which it attains in modern Socialism.

CHAPTER XV.

THE FALL OF THE GIRONDE.

APART from the laws referred to in the last chapter, which were with difficulty forced through the Legislature by the Mountain, the six weeks which elapsed between the acquittal of Marat and the 2nd of June, the day of the extinction of the Girondist power, were fruitful in nothing but a progressive mutual exacerbation of the two parties. Petitions and deputations began to pour in praying for the expulsion and even condemnation of some twenty-two of the leading Girondists. On the 10th of May the Convention shifted its quarters from the old Riding School to the Tuileries. The avenues to the new Convention hall were continually blocked by *sans-culottes* (the breechless), the name given to the party of the people since the *emeute* of the 21st of June, 1792, when among other emblems a pair of black breeches had been paraded in token of the want of these commodities by the working-classes of France. At last the Girondins made up their minds for a dashing stroke. Guadet suddenly moved the immediate suppression of the Commune, its place to be filled *ad interim* by the presidents of the sections, the transference of the legislation to Bourges with the smallest possible delay, and the despatch of the decree into the provinces by expresses. The Mountain was taken unawares, and it is possible, if the Girondists had had the courage to proceed to action immediately, they might have been successful. But this they did not dare do in face of the urgency of the

situation on the frontier, well knowing that civil war
would be the outcome. Indeed, it is doubtful whether
they could have in any case obtained a majority in the
Assembly under the circumstances. Barrére proposed,
as a compromise, the establishment of a commission of
twelve members to enquire into the conduct of the
municipality, to search out the plots of the Jacobins,
and to arrest suspected persons. The proposition was
accepted, and the commission established. Under the
pretence of having discovered a new conspiracy it
immediately proceeded to imprison several prominent
persons, among them being the secretary of the Commune, Hébert, editor of the *Père Duchesne* newspaper.
This at once excited immense popular indignation.
Deputation followed deputation demanding Hébert's
release. The Commune, the Mountainist mayor, Pache,
at its head, placed itself in permanent connection with
the committees of the sections, which, together with the
clubs of the Jacobins and Cordeliers, declared themselves
in permanent session.

On the 27th of May, the rising of Paris against the
Convention began. The Commune presented itself before
the Convention in a body, demanding the release of Hébert,
its chief secretary, and the suppression of the Girondist
Commission. Deputies from the sections followed, all
calling for its suppression, and some for the arrest of its
members. The Girondist president, Isnard, met these
demands with the threat that the departments should be
raised and Paris annihilated, so that " the wayfarer would
·have to enquire on which side of the Seine Paris had
stood," a reply which became the signal for a general
revolt of the Mountain.

The hall was now the scene of violent confusion, in
which swords and pistols were drawn, and during which
the crowd poured in, the upshot being that Isnard was
compelled to leave the chair and make way for the
Mountainist and friend of Danton, Hérault de Séchelles.

Hérault at once replied, conceding the demands of the petitioners.

The Mountain had won the day; Hébert's arrest was annulled, and the commission suppressed amid the acclamation of the populace. The next day the Girondists, with suicidal folly, succeeded by a scratch majority in re-establishing the Commission on the ground that the proceedings of the previous day had been irregular. A veritable yell of indignation from clubs, sections, and municipality greeted this resolution. Robespierre, Danton, Marat, Chaumette, and Pache constituted themselves into an informal committee to organise anew the movement. On the 30th, the clubs and sections publicly declared themselves in a state of insurrection, their delegates, to the number of ninty-six, entering the Hotel de Ville, and as a matter of form annulling the municipality (as a legally constituted body), but immediately reinstating its members in their functions under insurrectionary auspices. Mayor Pache was sent to report the matter to the Convention, while Henriot, the new commandant of the National Guard, called upon the sections to be ready for action at any moment, the *sansculottes* to be allowed two francs a-day so long as they remained under orders. Early the following morning, the 31st, the *tocsin* was rung and the *générale* beat, and the armed sections were assembled and marched upon the Tuileries.

The signal for the insurrection was an alarm cannon which was fired just as Mayor Pache was making his report, and, it must be admitted, trying to hoodwink the legislature with the pretence that he was not privy to the proceedings. The consternation in the assembly at the ominous sound was general. Danton rushed to the tribune to demand anew the suppression of the Commission. All the leading Mountainists did the same. The majority still hesitated. Deputations now began to arrive thick and fast, till all the gangways were blocked

E

up by excited crowds. The suppression of the Commission and the arrest of its members, and of the other leading Girondists, was loudly demanded on all sides. Various propositions were being discussed when the report spread that the Tuileries was surrounded by armed forces and the Convention no longer free. Even some members of the Mountain winced at this " outrage " on the " national sovereignty." At length it was decided that the Assembly should march out in a body and confront the insurgents. This was done, Hérault de Séchelles leading the way. They were met by Henriot on horseback at the head of the armed bands, brandishing a sabre. " The people want not phrases," he said, " but the arrest of twenty-two traitors."

Two cannons were immediately pointed straight at the Convention, which prudently retired. All the other exits from the Tuileries Gardens were found to bristle equally with pikes and sabres, so there was nothing for it but to go back again into the hall. The popular demands were no longer opposed. Marat, who had been the life and soul of the whole movement throughout, now dictated the names of the proscribed and the form of the resolution, from the tribune. All the leading Girondins, including the twelve forming the Commission, were placed under arrest. Upon the result being known outside, the insurgents quickly dispersed. Thus perished Girondism. Ever since the 10th of August, the nominal power in the State had been in the hands of the Girondist party; although, as we have seen, the real power was very far from being so. Henceforth they were a proscribed faction, whose members at last thought themselves lucky if they could find a corner of France in which to conceal themselves.

CHAPTER XVI.

THE SANSCULOTTE IN POWER.

THE Girondists, driven successively from the Municipality, the Jacobins' Club, the Ministry, and finally from the Convention, now played out their last card, the attempt to raise the Provinces, which were largely with them. Never was the position of France more desperate than at this moment. "La Vendée" in open and hitherto successful insurrection on one side, the coalition of Europe again pouring in its levies on three sides, and a Girondist insurrection brewing at several points in the interior. The Girondists, after their defeat in Paris, tried to rally at Caen, in Normandy, which town became the head-quarters of the conspiracy as long as it lasted. Negotiations were entered into with General Wimpfen and a Royalist, one Comte Puisaye. Somehow, in spite of the sympathy of the departments, especially the large middle-class towns, the project failed completely as a general movement, partly owing to mismanagement, want of concert and Royalist intrigues, which alienated many otherwise sympathetic, partly to the presence of the foreign invader, and partly to the vigorous action of the leaders of the Revolution in Paris. The provinces hesitated, the insurgents dispersed, a few towns in the south only remaining to the Girondins. · The insurrection did not miscarry for want of tall talk, it is certain, for the Girondins as usual were eloquent in threats couched in well-rounded periods.

While this was going on a young woman of "good"

family in Caen, who had been largely in the society of Girondins, and had heard much talk of Marat as the leader of the recent movement, without stating her intention to anybody, travelled up to Paris by *diligence*, and obtaining an interview with the popular leader under the pretext of furnishing information of the conspiracy at Caen, murdered him. Poor Marat, who was almost dying at the time, was in a bath, his helpless condition rendering him an easy prey to the knife of his dastardly assassin. A few sous only were found in his possession.

Thus perished the first great vindicator of the rights of the modern Proletariat, a truly single-minded champion of the oppressed. Of average intellect merely, it is Marat's unique and titanic force of character which must make him immortal in history.

Charlotte Corday was tried and condemned before the revolutionary tribunal, maintaining a theatrical demeanour to the last. She was guillotined on the 17th of July, three days after the assassination. A poor fool, a native of Mainz, Adam Lutz by name, went crazy over her.

The death of the "people's friend" caused a veritable panic in the ranks of the revolutionary party. No "patriot" was without some token of him. He was invoked in every revolutionary function, and his bust was crowned in all public assemblies. The Convention unanimously granted him the honours of the Pantheon. The fugitive Girondins now found their position harder than ever. They had to fly from Caen before the emissaries of the Mountain. Jacobin commissioners were scouring the country up and down, the revolutionary power in Paris having developed an almost superhuman activity. The only places where the insurrection still flickered on was in Lyons, Marseilles, and Bordeaux, cities which had compromised themselves too far, to hope for forgiveness from the Convention, and

which (notably Lyons) were destined before long to feel
the heavy hand of Sansculottic vengeance.

Yet notwithstanding the virtual collapse of the Girondist rebellion the state of affairs had hardly improved.
The armies, now again everywhere on the defensive, were
disorganised and dispirited. Things still seemed utterly
hopeless. If France was to be saved it could only be by
a dead lift. The revolutionary power in Paris now consisted of the Convention (or rather the Mountain, which
dominated the whole assembly), the two committees (of
General Security and of Public Safety), the Commune,
or Municipality, and, lastly, the clubs of the Jacobins
and Cordeliers, especially the former, whose deliberations
were hardly second in importance to those of the Convention. The primary assemblies of the forty-eight
sections, in which every citizen was free to express his
opinion, but which were almost entirely appropriated by
the Sansculottes, together with the "revolutionary committees" attached to them, were also a considerable
factor in public affairs.

This agglomeration of popular forces constituted the
power which had to raise France and the Revolution out
of the abyss into which they had sunk. The consolida-
tion of the new government was the first thing to be
attempted. The long-talked-of Constitution was next
put in hand, Hérault de Séchelles being entrusted with
the task of drawing it up. This celebrated Constitution
of '93, for long regarded as the sheet-anchor of Sansculottism, is probably the most thoroughgoing scheme
of pure democracy ever devised. It not only formally
recognised the people as the sole primary source of power,
but it delegated the exercise of that power directly to
them. Every measure was to be submitted to the
primary assemblies of the "sections," of which there
were forty-four thousand in all France. The magistrates
were to be re-elected at the shortest possible intervals by
simple majority. The central legislature was to be renewed annually, consisting of delegates from the primary

assemblies, who were to be furnished with imperative mandates.

This Constitution passed the Convention, and was accepted by a large majority of the " sections " throughout France. The representatives of the said forty-four thousand wardships, when they came to the Convention, demanded, in face of the existing emergency, " the arrest of all suspected persons and a general rising of the people." Danton, in a vigorous speech, moved that the commissioners of the primary assemblies should be instructed to report the state of arms, provisions, and ammunition, and to raise a levy of four hundred thousand men, and that the Convention should take the oath of death or victory. This was carried unanimously. A few days after, Barrere, in the name of the Committees, proposed still more decisive measures. All the male population, from eighteen to forty, were placed under arms, and new requisitions were made. Soon there were forty armies, comprising in all 1,200,000 men. The Committee of Public Safety, with Carnot (grandfather of the present President of the French Republic) as chief of the War Department, were untiring in their energies in organising the defence. Forty sous a day was enacted as the allowance of every Sectionist. The famous Law of Suspects was passed, and wholesale arrests were made of persons thought to be of Girondist or Royalist sympathies. The middle-classes fared now as badly as the aristocracy had previously. The reign of terror had begun, necessitated by the same exigencies as the September massacres—imminent foreign invasion combined with domestic treachery. As before, the moment decisive action was taken, matters began to mend on all sides, for though Toulon was in the hands of the English, Marseilles and Bordeaux were taken from the Girondin insurgents, and Lyons besieged. The Constitution, although carried, was suspended in face of the emergency, and, as a matter of fact, was never put into force.

CHAPTER XVII.

THE Revolutionary power in Paris, as we have said, was nominally divided between the Commune, at the head of which were Hébert and Chaumette, the two committees, which included Robespierre, Danton, Carnot, &c., the Convention, and the popular clubs, whose influence, though unofficial and indirect, was in no respect less than that of the representative assembly itself. During the period from August 10th, 1792, to the opening of the Convention (21st Sept.), the chief centre of power lay with the Commune led by Danton; from the 21st of September to the 2nd of June, the Convention, as a body, was more or less dominant; in the period from the 2nd of June, 1793, to the end of the year, power resided mainly in the Commune, led by the Hébertists; thenceforward to the 27th of July, 1794 (the fall of Robespierre), it was the committees, especially the Committee of Public Safety, which practically dictated to France. The Jacobins' Club meanwhile reflected for the most part the attitude of the dominant Parisian opinion, and of the governing body. It underwent several *épurations*, or purifications, in the course of the revolutionary period, on which occasions a batch of members, whose views were out of accord with the prevalent feeling of the hour, would be expelled.

Almost simultaneously with the collapse of the Girondist rising and the entry of the Convention troops into the cities of the south, the tide began to turn in La Vendée; the attempt of the insurgents to take Nantes failed, and though the insurrection lingered on for some time longer it never again became formidable. The revolutionary armies, indeed, were nearly everywhere victorious under the new generals, Moreau, Hoche, Pichegru, Jourdan, Kellermann, &c. The Prussians and Austrians, under the command of the Prince of Coburg, were dislodged from their vantage-ground in the east; the Spaniards driven back in the south, and the English and Hanoverians defeated in the north. Thus a second time was France, by a stupendous dead-lift effort, saved from imminent ruin by the raw levies of the Revolution.

The victories of Dumouriez in '92 were repeated on a grander scale in the great campaign, which the genius of Carnot "organised" in '93 and '94. The Revolution now was answering the coalition in the spirit of Danton's defiant menace "the combined kings threatens us, we hurl at their feet as guage of battle the head of a king." France was converted into one vast camp. But for many months yet the French were not destined to feel themselves "out of the wood." The dread of possible reverses followed by invasion and political extinction was ever before their eyes. And hence it was not till the end of July, '94, that the reaction against the "Terror" had gathered strength enough to overthrow the system itself. So long as danger threatened from without, public opinion tolerated the guillotine, and at the period at which we have arrived, the great activity of that famous instrument began. The "law of the suspect," which enabled the committees of the sections to arrest all suspected persons and incarcerate them prior to their being brought before the revolutionary tribunal, speedily filled the prisons to overflowing. After conviction and death the property of the executed was confiscated to the State.

The Commune was the virtual head of the revolutionary committees of the sections in the provinces as well as in Paris. It had a special force of 7,000 men, commanded by Ronsin, the dramatist, and called the "Revolutionary Army," under its orders, besides flying columns in its pay scouring different parts of the country. The Commune may be taken as the representative in the Revolution of the proletarian interest, pure and simple. Though the circumstances of the time caused it to be, unhappily, an instrument of the Terror, its activity was by no means confined to this. The Commune made it pretty soon evident than in its eyes the existence of a commercial middle-class was quite as incompatible with the welfare of the people as that of an aristocracy.

Economical equality was the avowed end of the Revolution for the Commune. Hébert and Chaumette, nevertheless, busied themselves with various projects of a palliative character, such as hospital and prison reform. They attempted to introduce primary and secular education into every village in France. The law of *maximum* (and compulsory sale) was at their suggestion enlarged in scope, being applied to almost all articles of common consumption. Forestalling was forbidden under the heaviest penalties. A maximum was even applied to wages at this time, a proceeding calculated in a society not yet out of the small production to make considerable havoc with what some people call the "rent of ability," though it was enacted solely with a view to government employment for the national defence. The Bourse was closed. Financial and commercial syndicates were dissolved. The paper money, or *assignats*, were made compulsory tender at their nominal value.

On the 5th of October the new Republican calendar, the joint work of the astronomer Romme, who furnished the calculations, and the clever feuilletonist, Fabre d'Eglantine, who supplied the poetical nomenclature, came into operation. The new era was to date from the declaration of the Republic, the 21st of September, 1792, so that the months do not coincide with those of the ordinary calendar. The three autumn months were *Vendémiaire*, or the vintage month, *Brumaire*, or the foggy month, and *Frimaire*, or the frosty month; the three winter months, *Nivose*, or the snowy month, *Pluviose*, or the rainy month, and *Ventose*, or the windy month; the three spring months, *Germinal*, or the budding month, *Forêal*, or the flowery month, and *Prairial*, or the meadowy month; and the three summer months, *Messidor*, or the reaping month, *Thermidor*, or the heating month, and *Fructidor*, or the fruiting month. The week of seven days was abolished and decades or periods of ten days instituted instead.

But the work for which the Commune is most famous is the establishment of the new Cultus—the Worship of Reason. The Hébertists, as the party of the Commune were now called, and among whom was Anacharsis Clootz, were firmly convinced that deliverance from the dogmas of supernatural religion was the necessary complement of deliverance from the thraldom of privilege and wealth. In accordance with 18th century habits of thought, especially in France with its classicism, the idea naturally suggested itself of initiating a worship of Reason as personified, on the ruins of God, Christ, and the Virgin. For some time past, stimulated by the missionaries of the Commune, numbers of priests had been sending in their demissions, declaring they would no longer preach a lie, and that Liberty and the public welfare were their only gods. The church plate in every part of France was melted down for patriotic uses, vestments, bibles, and breviaries made bonfires, to the accompaniment of the "Carmagnole." Early in November Gobel, the Archbishop of Paris, together with his chapter, entered the Convention hall to publicly renounce the Christian faith. Christian rites and worship were now proscribed, and a Festival of Reason was decreed by the Commune at the instance of Chaumette. A few days later, and a procession of citizens and citizenesses, in priestly vestments, and other fantastic costumes, followed by mules and barrows laden with church furniture, defiled into the Convention, and after chanting strophes to Reason, proceeded to dance

the "Carmagnole," many of the legislators taking part.
Later on the same day, Procureur Chaumette, at the
head of the Commune and the presidents of sections,
arrived bearing in their midst, on a palaquin, Mdlle.
Candeille, the *danseuse*, in *bonnet rouge* and blue mantle,
garlanded with oak as the Goddess of Reason.   The
bulk of the Convention then rose, and after giving the
goddess the formal kiss, proceeded in a body to Notre
Dame, where the new worship was inaugurated amid
music, tricolour, and virgins dressed in white.   A similar
ceremony with other goddesses took place at St. Eustache,
and other of the principal churches of Paris.   Commissioners soon established the new worship throughout the
length and breadth of French territory, from Antwerp
in the north to Marseilles in the south.   In place of the
Mass the old cathedrals re-echoed to strophes in honour
of Reason and in praise of "Liberty, Equality, and Fraternity."   Over the churchyards appeared the device,
"Death is an eternal sleep."   Old things had passed
away, and all things had become new.   It should be
said that the "Goddess of Reason" was never intended to
be more than a symbol, and not as has been sometimes
represented, herself an object of worship.   Viewed in its
true light, the idea, if somewhat pedantic was not
unpleasing.

CHAPTER XVIII.

THE TERROR.

By means of its courageous contempt for the so-called laws of political economy, its wholesale requisitions and the compulsion exercised on all traders and farmers, with the aid of its "revolutionary army," to sell at the maximum price, the fearful misery occasioned by the circumstances of the time was kept under to a considerable extent by the Commune. The revolutionary committees established in every section of France, the ambulatory deputies who watched the provinces and were present with the military forces, and last, but not least, the army of the Commune under General Ronsin, nevertheless had hard work to prevent the law of maximum from being violated. The Commune now granted a free allowance of bread for each family. Arrests in Paris and the provinces went on apace. By the end of October 3,000 persons were in the prisons of Paris alone, the revolutionary committees formed in every section having, as already stated, power to arrest all persons suspected of reactionary tendencies.

On the 14th of October the queen, Marie Antoinette, was brought before the Revolutionary Tribunal and convicted, after two days' hearing, on overwhelming evidence, of the basest treachery towards France, and of the most sanguinary intentions with regard to Paris. It was, indeed, high time that this atrocious woman met her deserts. When the country was at the lowest depths of misery some years before the outbreak of the Revolution, all this abandoned wretch could think of was squandering fabulous sums of the nation's wealth, in conjunction with her friend, the Court head prostitute and procuress, the Princess de Lamballe (killed in the September massacres), on jewels, balls, and sinecures for her paramours. If anyone ventured to call attention to some flagrant abuse in her presence, he was invariably silenced with the reply, " Yes, but we must amuse ourselves " (" Oui, mais il faut s'amuser)." It was only after her amusements had been curtailed by the utter collapse of the finances, a consummation to which she had contributed so largely by her criminal extravagances, that she began to interest herself in public affairs. Her aim was then to get back the means for her debaucheries, and when the Revolution broke out and affairs looked less and less productive of diamond necklaces, &c., her hatred against the new régime which had deprived her of those things naturally knew no bounds, and henceforth her one hope was a foreign invasion, which would quench the Revolution in the blood of France, and place the French people once more in her power. As for poor, feeble, foolish Louis, he was completely in the toils of this noxious reptile.[1] Many who looked on at the tumbril conveying her to execution must have been inclined to think that the guillotine was too good for the foul *Autrichienne*.

She was not without a certain histrionic ability, and when before the tribunal played out her " queenly figure " in a manner which showed that she might have gained an honest living in transpontine melodrama. Much indignation has been expended on the charge of misconduct towards her son, the little dauphin, which Hébert brought against her. It is sufficient here to state that there are extant documents which show that the charge was not

---

[1] The real character of Maria Antoinette, apart from the lies of Royalist historians, may be seen from her correspondence with Maria-Theresa, and of the latter with the Comte Mercy D'Argenteau. A good digest of it is given in M. Georges Avenel's essay, " La Vrai Marie Antoinette."

made without very good grounds, although in the nature
of things it could not be certainly proved. The fact is,
it is a mistake to apply the ordinary canons of maternity
to a creature like Marie Antoinette. She was altogether
an obscene abortion of the corrupt court-life of the 18th
century, the like of which, let us hope, may never be seen
again.

Apropos of the dauphin, it is necessary to caution our
readers against the lies of the reaction anent his treatment, and especially the foul calumnies against the
young shoemaker, Simon, in whose care he was placed.
All the contemporary evidence goes to show that the
poor child received every consideration and kindness, but
that having inherited a scrofulous or syphillitic constitution from both parents, which was further weakened
in ways unnecessary to go into, it was impossible to rear
him, that in spite of every care he died in the Temple
the following year.

On the 24th of October the 22 Girondists were brought
to trial. They were convicted after five days' proceedings, and guillotined on the sixth. Valazé, one of
their number, stabbed himself to death with a dagger on
hearing the sentence, but his body was nevertheless sent
to be guillotined with the rest. They embraced each other
on arriving at the " Place de la Revolution," and died
singing the " Marseillaise." Proofs of their complicity in
the insurrection of the departments were complete.
They had played for high stakes and lost. Seventy-
three other Girondist deputies had been for some time
under lock and key, having been compromised in some
papers found at the house of a deputy whom Charlotte
Corday had visited on her first arrival in Paris. With
the execution of the twenty-two, however, Girondism, as
a distinct party, finally disappears from history. The
Girondins, it may here be mentioned, were largely under
the influence of Voltaire, just as the Mountain as a party
was chiefly under the influence of Rousseau.

Meanwhile Lyons, the last stronghold of Royalism and Girondism, had fallen, and Toulon had been recovered from the English, to whom it had been surrendered. Both towns were visited with a fearful vengeance. Collot d'Herbois, who was a member both of the Commune and of the Committee of Public Safety, acting in conjunction with Couthon, the disciple of Robespierre, ordered wholesale massacres of the inhabitants of the former city in his capacity of Commissioner. Billaud-Varennes, a colleague of Collot's, was also a leading agent of the terror. Lebon worked the guillotine at Arras. Fréron the Dantonist made his holocausts at Marseilles and Toulouse, and Tallien at Bordeaux. At Nantes, Carrier, another Commissioner, inaugurated his horrible *Noyades*, or drownings, in which those suspected of Royalism or Moderatism were placed in boats with false bottoms and drowned in the Loire. In some of these cases a man and woman were tied together naked. This was called "Republican marriage." The Revolutionary Commissioners or Pro-Consuls in some cases travelled from town to town carrying a guillotine with them. All these things were very infamous, it will be said, and so they were. But they were not any worse, if so bad, as the acts of more than one respectable government in '48, of the Czar in Poland in '63, or of the Versaillists in Paris in '71, events which the middle-classes have complacently swallowed without indignation!

CHAPTER XIX.

THE FALL OF THE HÉBERTISTS.

AFTER the 10th of August and the events that arose out of it of which he was the heart and soul, Danton had proved something of a failure. His peace negociations with England had led to nothing, his attempts at reconciliation between Mountain and Gironde had likewise proved abortive; he had played no important part since the 2nd of June in the Convention itself, and finally retired with his young wife for some weeks in disgust to his native town of Arcis sur Aube, whence he returned some time after to join his friend Camille Desmoulins in attacking the system of the terror. It should be explained that the Cordeliers' Club, of which Danton had formerly been the head, had been reconstituted some time since, and was now entirely composed of Hébertists. Camille, at the beginning of December, started a new journal called "The Old Cordelier," which attacked the Terrorists, and especially the Commune, with bitter sarcasm. At first Robespierre approved of the sentiments there expressed, and even looked over and corrected the proofs of the first numbers. It pleased him that the Hébertists were sharply attacked. For the pedantic Rousseauite prig Robespierre was mortally offended with the atheism of the party of the Commune, and had recently been delivering violent harangues against the worship of Reason, at the Jacobins' Club. Robespierre, who was ambitious of being the Washington of France, and had set his mind upon getting himself recognised by the powers, wished to pose before them as the moderate man opposed to excesses of every description, and thereby to win them over. There was also an old-standing jealousy on the part of the Committee of Public Safety with the Commune on account of the influence the latter wielded with the aid of its "revolutionary army."

Nevertheless, Robespierre's two colleagues on the committee, Billaud Varennes and Collot D'Herbois, were enraged at the idea of even mitigating the "Terror," and the notion found but little support generally. Robespierre, whose influence was now immense, became suddenly alarmed lest he should be tarred with moderation, and hence a coolness sprang up between him and his friend Camille and the other Dantonists.

Meanwhile the guillotine was working steadily every day, and some noteworthy heads were falling or had lately fallen. Among them we may notice Philippe D'Orleans Egalité, the ex-member of the Mountain and the king's cousin, arrested at the time Dumouriez's intrigues with his son became known, and decreed accused along with the Girondins, but not convicted till later. In November, Madame Roland was also put on her trial. She was condemned, and went to the Place de la Revolution by the side of a poor printer, whom she endeavoured to console. Arrived there, she asked for paper and ink to write down "the strange thoughts that were arising within her." Madame Roland was a remarkable woman, but even apart from her politics, one is repelled by her perpetual pedantry and posing, and still more by her venomous hatred and malignant calumnies against her opponents. She was an *intrigueuse* of the first rank, and practically led the tactics of the Girondist party.

Bailly, the first mayor of Paris under the new *régime*, him of the red flag of the Champ de Mars, in July, 1791, was one of the executed. Barnard, the Constitutionalist leader in the Constituent Assembly, also suffered. The corpse of the Girondist, Pétion, who succeeded Bailly in the mayoralty of Paris, was found about this time in a wood near St. Emilion, partly devoured by wolves. The heads of ex-ministers and generals were falling by the score.

But to return to the contest of parties in the government. Put in a few words, the matter stood as follows: on one side were the Hébertists, representing the Commune and the Terror; on the opposite were the Dan-

F

tonists, representing to a large extent the Convention
party, and hostile now to both the Commune and the
Terror, wishing to see the Constitution established and
the Convention all powerful. Between the two were
the committees, that of "public safety" being the dominant one. The committee-men were mostly hostile to the
power of the Commune, which stood in their way, but
were determined to maintain the system of the Terror,
and not to let the Convention override their authority.

Robespierre, after some hesitation, ranged himself on
the side of his committee alike against the Dantonists,
with whom he had, up till now, been friendly, and the
Hébertists, to whom he had been always more or less
hostile. The struggle lasted between three and four
months, and many were the stormy meetings of Jacobins,
Cordeliers, and "sections," anent this death-drama between
the Sansculottes, the Dantonists, and the committee-men.
Since the reconstitution of the Committee of Public
Safety in July, when Billaud and Collot came into
it, the Dantonists had had no influence on either of the
committees. The attack on the Hébertists was begun
by the suppression of the revolutionary armies in the
provinces, and a decree forbidding the sending of agents
into the provinces by the Commune, and this was followed
up inside and outside the Convention by concerted attacks
on every action of the Commune from the Dantonists, the
Mountain, and from the Committees. The Jacobins'
Club continued to be the battle-ground between Robespierre and the Hébertists. There Robespierre thundered
nightly against atheistic intolerance, said that Atheism
was aristocratic, on the ground that certain aristocrats
had been Atheists, omitting to recognise the fact that
they wished to retain Atheism and Freethought as an
exclusive privilege of their class. He maundered about
the necessity of a Supreme Being as the avenger of in-
jured innocence, and much more of a similar kind.

At last the compact between Robespierre and his fellow-
committee-men, Billaud and Collot, was struck. They were

to surrender their old friends the Hébertists, while he was to surrender the Dantonists. A projected insurrection inaugurated by the " section " called " Marat," in favour of the Hébertists, miscarried, owing to the failure to take action at the right moment. Accordingly Hébert, Ronsin, Vincent, Clootz, Momoro, and others, already expelled from the Jacobins' Club, were arrested, and after a mock trial, in which they were accused of taking money from the English Government to discredit the Republic by their excesses, were, on 24th March, 1794, sent to the guillotine. Poór Chaumette's turn came a few days later.

A week afterwards Danton, who had come back to Paris at the earnest solicitation of his friends, and had sought ineffectually to compromise matters with Robespierre, was sent before the revolutionary tribunal. This was Robespierre's great *coup*. Danton's personality, combined with his oratory, was nearly securing his acquittal, when Robespierre got a special law hurried through the Convention, which closed his mouth, and he, too, went his way in company with his friends Camille Desmoulins, Phillipeaux, Hérault, De Séchelles, and others, to the Place de la Revolution. Thus was the Revolution, indeed, like Saturn, devouring its own children.

When we first came across Robespierre, he was, although a prig, and a repulsive prig at that, apparently actuated by as much honesty of purpose as any other leader. His services to the Revolution at all the great crises were real. But the germ of ambition and personal self-seeking, which was always observable, grew with the progress of events, until, at the period we have now reached, he had developed into a monster, actuated by one aim—to become dictator, and prepared to make any sacrifice whatever for the accomplishment of that aim. The murder of friends like Danton and Desmoulins, with whom he had lived and worked on terms of close intimacy since the beginning of the Revolution, yields to nothing in history for its treachery and infamy.

CHAPTER XX.

THE RULE OF ROBESPIERRE.

THE old Commune was now overthrown, and all independence stifled in the Convention. No initiative remained but that of the Committee of Public Safety, and in the Committee itself little, at least in internal affairs, but that of Maximilian Robespierre and his partisans. The chief among the latter were Couthon and Lebas in Paris, and St. Just and Lebon as Commissioners in the provinces. The municipality, now that most of the old members were guillotined or expelled, was filled up with subordinate creatures of Robespierre. A Belgian architect, named Fleuriot-Lescot, replaced the devoted and noble-minded Pache as mayor of Paris. The same thing went on all round. The Cordelier's Club was suppressed. Robespierre had succeeded in reducing the Jacobins' Club to a mere *claque* of his own. The Convention was not much better. A look from the "Incorruptible" (as Robespierre was called) sufficed to frown down all opposition.

The increase of the Terror now became frightful all over France, but especially in Paris. Robespierre himself directed the police department. On the 22nd of Prairial (the 10th of June), an atrocious law was passed at the instigation of the dictator, whereby persons sent before the revolutionary tribunal, now divided into four sections, were refused the right of defence. This meant, of course, that whereas before about a third of those accused were acquitted, henceforth all prisoners were condemned, when nothing else could be alleged against them, on the general and vague charge of "conspiracies in the prisons." Men and women were now tried by the public prosecutor, Fouquier Tinville, and the judges of the Tribunal, in batches of fifty or sixty at once. It would be a mistake to suppose that it was chiefly the well-to-do that suffered. On the contrary, out of 2,750 victims of Robespierre's, only 650 belonged to the upper or middle-classes. The tumbrils that wended their way daily to the Place de la Revolution and afterwards to the Faubourg St. Antoine, were largely filled with working-men. During the last three weeks of the tyrant's rule, 1,125 persons were executed in Paris alone. Thus did this criminal monster drown the Revolution itself in the blood of his victims. Marat had already foreseen the results of Robespierre's self-idolatry, when during a speech of the latter in the Convention, he whispered to his neighbour, Dubois-Crancé,—" With such doctrines as that, he will do more harm than all the tyrants put together."

The notion of becoming the high-priest of a new religion had been working in Robespierre's mind ever since the fall of the Hébertists. After many speeches in the Jacobins' Club, on the 18th of May, Maximilian at last mounted the Convention tribune to demand that it be decreed that " the French people recognises the existence of a Supreme Being and the immortality of the soul," and that a festival should be held in honour of the said Being. In his speech he dwelt on the distinction between a pure Deism and the superstitious cults of priests, said that it mattered not whether the existence of God were demonstrable or even probable, that " in the eyes of the legislator all is truth which is useful in the world and in practice," that a god was an indispensable article of state-furniture, and much more to the same effect. Deputations from the new Robespierrised Commune, from the Jacobins, and from the sections next filed in with the petition that the Convention should vouchsafe to grant them a God and Immortality. The resolution was carried amid thunders of applause in the same Convention which six months previously had applauded the atheistic worship of Reason.

A few days afterwards, one undoubted, and another more questionable, attempt at assassination was made. The first on Collot D'Herbois, on the steps of his house ; and the second on Robespierre himself by a young woman named Cécilie Rénault. Robespierre was out when she called, but she was arrested, and knives were found in her possession.   She was guillotined, together with all her family.   Fifty-four persons, dressed in red smocks, were involved in this execution, which took place in the Faubourg St. Antoine, the great workmen's quarter.

At last the eventful day, the 20th of Prairial (8th of June), fixed for the glorification of the Supreme Being, arrived.   The Convention, the Jacobins, and Sections in gala attire, might have been seen wending their way, in splendid summer weather, through the Tuileries' Gardens, the procession headed by Robespierre, radiant in sky-blue coat and black breeches, bearing in his hand an enormous bunch of corn, fruits, and flowers, a classical touch suggested by the pagan functions of antiquity. Arrived at an improvised altar, on the top of which were allegorical figures intended to represent Atheism, Anarchy, &c., Robespierre proceeded to set fire to the latter with a torch.   They blazed away, and presently by a triumph of mechanical art the Supreme Being himself emerged from their ashes, rather the worse for smoke, it is said. The "Incorruptible" made three harangues, but the hopes of those who expected an announcement of a cessation of the Terror were damped when he proclaimed : "To-day let us enjoy ourselves, to-morrow begin afresh to fight the enemies of the Revolution."   All knew what this meant, and two days later the monstrous law before spoken of was passed, and the Terror entered upon its last and acutest stage.

This disappointment of the public hopes was the be-

ginning of the fall of Robespierre's popularity outside the
governing bodies. Suppressed hatred and jealousy of
him had long been the growing feeling in the Convention,
while on the Committee of Public Safety he had become
at loggerheads with all except his own henchmen. The
law of Prairial was the last occasion that the Committee
appeared united before the Convention. Fouquier Tinville,
the public prosecutor, went to the Committee himself to
complain of the new law as being the *reductio ad
absurdum* of the Terror, and was told that it had been
yielded under protest to Robespierre's importunity. So
strained were the relations, that Robespierre henceforth
rarely attended the sittings of the Committee, and appeared comparatively seldom in the Convention itself,
leaving everything to Couthon, St. Just, and Lebas. On
the other hand, he was assiduous in his attendance at the
Jacobins'. He never went out of doors, indeed, now, without an escort of Jacobins armed with bludgeons. An incident occurred about this time which was dexterously used
by his enemies to throw ridicule upon the high-priest and
would-be dictator. A crazy woman named Catherine
Théot, calling herself the Mother of God, proclaimed the
advent of a Messiah, and in conjunction with an ex-priest
set up a kind of free-masonic society. Barrére, the
dexterous trimmer, drew up a clever report on the subject, in which he hinted at Robespierre's desiring to profit
by the proceedings of the fanatics without naming him.
Billaud, Collot, and the members o the "Committee of
General Safety," who had been attached to the old Commune, and were partisans of the Worship of Reason, had
taken offence at the cultus of the Supreme Being. "You
and your Supreme Being," Billaud was heard to say in a
stage-aside on the occasion, "are beginning to bore me."
It was now, therefore, a case of "aut Cæsar aut nullus,"
with Robespierre.

CHAPTER XXI.

THERMIDOR.

It had become a matter of life and death to Robespierre to overthrow the hostile members of the committees and get himself recognised as dictator. St. Just tried it on on behalf of his friend several times with the "Public Safety," but without effect. St. Just, by the way, was probably the most sincere and enthusiastic of all the followers of Robespierre. Not yet twenty-five years of age, he had made a great mark on the Revolution. His large, poetic eyes, his tall and dignified figure, his long dark hair, had obtained for him the nickname of the "apocalyptic." It was necessary to take action without delay. The whole of the Committee of General Security and the majority of the Committee of Public Safety were against Robespierre. The Convention therefore had to be tried, and failing the Convention an insurrection proclaimed, headed by the Jacobins and the Commune. The latter bodies were prepared some time beforehand to resort to force if necessary to the ends of their champion, and a conspiracy was actually formed, the leaders of which were St. Just, Couthon, who, together with Robespierre, constituted the so-called triumvirate, the Mayor Fleuriot, the "national agent" Payan, Dumas, the president, and Coffinhal, the vice-president of the Revolutionary Tribunal. St. Just had been recalled in great haste by Robespierre from his mission with the army of the North, and when apprised of the state of affairs he advised an immediate *coup d'état*. This, however, was impracticable. The Convention had to be sounded first, otherwise the pretext for rising was wanting. Accordingly, early on the 26th of July (8th of Thermidor) Robespierre repaired to the Assembly and opened the sitting with a long and dexterous speech, denouncing the Committees and defending himself in the name of the national sovereignty. He wound up by recommending a general " purification " all round of the Committees and of the Convention.

Robespierre sat down amid absolute silence. Not a sound or word of applause greeted his challenge. Presently, a member, Lecointre, rose and moved the printing and circulation of the harangue. This was at once vigorously resisted, but was eventually carried.

The members of the two Committees, hitherto silent, now took up the challenge. They attacked Robespierre in turn. The upshot was that the decree for the printing and circulation of the discourse was virtually rescinded, being referred to the Committees for examination. Robespierre, surprised at the unwonted resistance, left the sitting discouraged, but without despairing of the situation.

In the evening he repaired to the Jacobins', when he re-read the discourse of the morning, and here it was, of course, greeted with tumultous applause. The Committees, on their side, kept together all night. Nothing was omitted during these momentous hours by either party to ensure victory on the morrow. The Committees and the Mountain negociated successfully with the Plain to bring about common action in the Assembly. Before noon the following day, July 27th (9th Thermidor), members were to be seen encouraging each other in the corridors. The sitting was opened by St. Just. He had scarcely begun his speech, attacking the Committees, when he was interrupted and denounced by the ex-commissioner Tallien, who demanded that " the veil should be withdrawn from the conspiracy." Tallien was supported on all sides. Billaud Varennes then spoke of " packed " meetings of Jacobins, of threats against the representatives, &c.   At this point of Billaud's speech the whole Convention rose and swore to defend the national sovereignty amid the applause of the public in the galleries.   All eyes were now turned towards Robespierre, who finally made a dash at the tribune.   Before he could speak, however, the cry of " Down with the tyrant ! " resounded throughout the hall.

Tallien, in an uncompromising speech, then demanded the arrest of Henriot, the commander of the reconstituted armed force of Paris, Billaud, the arrest of other partisans of Robespierre, measures which were at once acceded to.

Robespierre repeatedly attempted to defend himself, but his voice was always drowned with shouts of " Down with the tyrant ! " and by the ringing of the President's bell.   He turned to the " Plain," he turned to the public in the galleries, there was no response from either.   Finally he sank down on a seat, exhausted, and foaming at the mouth.

" The blood of Danton chokes the wretch," cried a member of the Mountain.

Robespierre's arrest was demanded on all sides.   His brother, Augustin Robespierre, Couthon, Lebas, and St. Just all claimed to share his fate, and were finally all given into the hands of the gendarmerie.   The moment this became known at the Hotel de Ville, where the Mayor, Payan, and Henriot were assembled with the Commune, orders were given for the barriers to be closed, the sections assembled, the *tocsin* sounded, the *générale* beaten, and the insurrection proclaimed.   The ca noncers were ordered to repair to the Place de Grève by the Hotel de Ville, and the Revolutionary Committees were sent for to take the oath of insurrection.   The arrested deputies had meanwhile been released by their partisans, on their way to the prisons, and brought in triumph to the Hotel de Ville.

The Jacobins, who declared themselves in permanent

session, formed a subordinate centre of insurrection. Henriot, who then rushed through the streets, pistol in hand, calling on the people to rise, was seized by two deputies, and was being brought to the Committees, when he was liberated by Coffinhal, at the head of two hundred cannoneers, of which Henriot himself at once took the command, placing them in position round the Convention.

The Assembly, which had adjourned for a couple of hours, had now reassembled. It was seven o'clock. "Citizens," said the President, "now is the time for us to die at our post." Affairs did certainly look hopeless for the Convention. Orders were almost immediately given by Henriot to fire, when, strange to say, the cannoneers, who, up to this time, had been with the insurgents, hesitated, wavered, and finally refused to comply. In the hands of those two hundred cannoneers lay the fate of France. Henriot hurried off to the Hotel de Ville. It was now the turn of the Convention to take the aggressive. The response of the sections to the call of the Commune was not altogether satisfactory. The fact is, the movement of the last two days had been sudden even for Paris, and had developed out of a quarrel inside the government, with which the general public were imperfectly acquainted. Besides this, Robespierre's unpopularity had now become general. Though the sections assembled at nine o'clock, they confined themselves to sending messages to the Commune, asking for further information.

While the assembled sections were discussing the matter in the various wards of the city, delegates from the Convention arrived apprising them of the real position of affairs. They now no longer hesitated, but arming themselves, immediately proceeded, not to the Place de Grève, but to the Tuileries, where they were naturally received with great enthusiasm. A small body, with a few pieces of artillery, having been left as a guard to the Convention, the remainder then marched off to attack the head centre of the insurrection—the Hotel de Ville. The crowds which had assembled outside at the sound of the *tocsin* had gradually dispersed, finding the sections did not arrive, and the space was now much thinned. Emissaries from the Convention proclaimed the outlawry of the insurgents, upon which all that remained went home.

The armed sections now arrived from the Tuileries, occupied all the outlets, and set up a prolonged shout of " Long live the Convention ! " The insurgents saw at once that all was lost. Robespierre shot himself, but only succeeded in breaking his jaw. His brother threw himself from the third story. Lebas killed himself with a pistol. Couthon mangled himself with a knife. Coffinhal pitched Henriot from the window into the common sewer and managed to escape. St. Just alone awaited his fate with dignity and calmness.

It was now about one o'clock in the morning. The conspirators were conducted first to the Committee of General Security. Robespierre lay on a litter suffering horribly, exposed to the jeers and taunts of the bystanders, who upbraided him with all his crimes. They were afterwards taken to the prison of the Conciergerie, and brought up thence the next day before the Revolutionary Tribunal, with others of their associates. They were, of course, condemned, and were executed the same evening at six o'clock. Immense crowds, hooting and jeering, thronged the streets to see the tumbrils as they passed. Uncomplimentary references to the Supreme Being and to the prospective immortality of Robespierre's soul were not wanting. A halt was made before the house where Robespierre had lodged. All eyes were turned on him in his " Supreme Being " blue coat, and the jeers and invectives grew louder. The sullen hatred which had been growing for weeks past suddenly found vent. At the time of his fall he probably had scarcely two or three hundred real followers in all Paris.

Instead of mitigating or abolishing the Terror at the moment, when, the danger of invasion being past, it had

Instead of mitigating or abolishing the Terror at the moment, when, the danger of invasion being past, it had no longer any solid backing in public opinion, he had chosen to exascerbate it, only too obviously for his own ambitious purposes. Thus he speedily degenerated from the most popular to the most hated man in all France. The battle of Fleurus on the 26th of June had secured for France the re-conquest of Belgium, and destroyed the last remaining chance of foreign invasion; and hence, all but the blind followers of the system were determined to be rid of the Terror, the national extremity which gave rise to it having passed away.

Robespierre was the last to ascend the scaffold. As Samson the executioner wrenched off the bloody linen which bound up his jaw, a horrible yell escaped him. This was the only sign of life since his arrest. The moment his head fell, a roar of applause, which lasted some minutes, resounded far and wide on the evening air. Such was the celebrated Revolution of "Thermidor."

CHAPTER XXII.

THE REACTION BEGINS.

IT is plain to us now that the fall of Robespierre meant the end of the Terror, although the partisans of the system on the Committees could not see it. The Billaud Varennes, Collot D'Herbois, and Barréres thought still to carry on the proscriptions with the other methods of revolutionary government. They lost influence every day. The Terror was at once abolished, except for the "tail" of Robespierre, the members of the Commune, some of the leading Robespierrists, Jacobins, &c., who were guillotined to the number of some hundred and fifty in a few days. In the relief which "Sansculottes" like the rest felt at being rid of the perpetual Damocles' sword of Tinville, and of the endless rant about "virtue," "austerity," "incorruptibility," with which Robespierre and his crew had sickened everyone, they little thought that the end of the Revolution itself, in so far as it interested the working classes of France, was at hand. In truth, the reaction had begun four months before, with the destruction of the party of the old Commune— the Hébertists. When a Revolution proceeds to exterminate its most enthusiastic adherents its fate is obviously sealed. Robespierre had denounced the Hébertists as Atheists and Communists. To the inventor of the "Supreme Being" and the "Declaration of Rights," which was foisted upon the Jacobins in opposition to Chaumette and Hébert, and according to which "the right of property is the right of every citizen to enjoy and dispose as he pleases of his goods," which provided also that "no commerce should be prohibited," and no property ever confiscated even for public purposes "without indemnity" —to such a one the Hébertists were offensive without doubt.

What Robespierre desired was, in short, a Republic of starched, middle-class prigs, of which he himself was to be the type. The Hébertists, especially men like Chaumette and Anacharsis Clootz, whatever their faults may have been, at least desired a change better worth fighting for than this. Their instincts were Socialistic though their ideas may have been vague, as they could scarcely fail to have been a century ago, when the "great industry" had hardly begun. As to the Terror, Robespierre substituted for the irregular methods of the Commune a systematic plan of butchery, which enabled him to rid himself conveniently of personal enemies. Still, even Robespierre, in spite of their contradicting the free trade principles he had laid down, did not dare to suggest abolishing the *maximum* and other measures passed under the influence of the Commune for ensuring a possible livelihood to the working classes. This it was reserved for the Thermidorians to do.

The Committee-men had accepted the aid of the Convention in overthrowing Robespierre and his party. They soon found that the Convention was as determined to rid itself of the dictatorship of the Committees as the Committees themselves had been that of Robespierre. The very next day the Committees began to be attacked. The abolition of the Revolutionary Tribunal was proposed. Barrére, who spoke in its support, was taunted with having been a Constitutional Royalist before the 10th of August. The Convention, nevertheless, confined itself this time to issuing a decree of accusation against Fonquier Tinville and abolishing the law of Prairial.

The Committees themselves were next reorganised and their power curtailed. The Paris Commune never again rose after its second defeat under Robespierre. The old suspects were gradually released from prison. But the reaction did not stop at abolishing the Terror. It began at once undoing all the "Sansculottic" work of the Revolution. First, the daily meetings of the sections were reduced to one in ten days. Next, the allowance of twenty sous a day for indigent members was done away with. Next, the *maximum* was abolished. The com-missioners Lebon and Carrier (the author of the *noyades* at Nantes) were now tried. Most of the old members of the Committees shortly after this either resigned or were ousted, and their places were filled with Thermidorians.

Fréron, the ex-Mountainist and now Reactionist, started a paper in which he proposed that the youth of the upper and middle classes should arm themselves with loaded sticks to resist the Sansculottes. The suggestion was eagerly adopted, and a new and fantastic dress was assumed as a counterblast to the *Carmagnole* costume of the popular party. An open-breasted front, long hair, done up behind in tresses, called *cadenettes*, and low shoes, formed the *costume à la victime* of the *Jeunesse dorée* (gilded youth), as they were called. Every day street fights took place between them and the Jacobins. The latter, though they had undergone one of their customary purifications after the fall of Robespierre, and had duly sent a deputation congratulating the Convention on the death of "the tyrant," found themselves daily getting into worse odour with the dominant party.

The Convention before long broke up the vast federa-tion of clubs of which the Paris Jacobins was the head by arbitrarily forbidding any further correspondence between the centre and the provincial branches. The Assembly, at the same time, declined to receive any further deputations. Nevertheless the club was still the rallying point of every revolutionary influence in Paris. An attempt was made to liberate Carrier, which, although unsuccessful, gave rise to a formidable disturbance, and led to the suspension of the Jacobin sittings by the Convention. The members assembled the next day notwithstanding, in defiance of the decree, but the meeting-place was attacked by the "gilded youth," and the Jacobins driven out. The Convention thereupon suppressed the club altogether (November 12).

The Thermidorian party at first wanted a revolutionary reputation to counterbalance that of Robespierre, and chose Marat, who, owing to the jealousy of the former, had not as yet received the honours of the Pantheon, which the Convention had granted after his death. But it was not long before the reputation of Marat, like everything else belonging to the Proletarian side of the Revolution, fell under the ban of the reactionary party, his busts were everywhere destroyed, and his name became the byeword it has been ever since, or at least until quite recently.

The decree of expulsion against the nobles and priests was now rescinded. The seventy-three members who had protested against the expulsion of the Girondins were released from prison and reinstated in their places in the Convention. The monument in front of the "Invalides," celebrating the victory of the Mountain over the Gironde, was destroyed. Soon after this the few remaining Girondist leaders who had come out of hiding were received back into the Convention, thus further strengthening the great "moderate party" which had formed out of the wreckage of various parties. In January, 1795, the churches were again opened for Christian worship, though here some caution was observed, a good many restrictions on religious propagandism being still maintained. The armies were now supplied solely by contract and not partially by requisitions on private property as heretofore. The confiscated goods of suspects and of those executed during the Terror were restored in the first instance to themselves, in the second to their nearest relations.

G

CHAPTER XXIII.

THE REACTION PROGRESSES.

THE reaction was daily growing in intensity. The fury of the new " White Terror" in Paris had reached other leaders than Carrier and Lebon, both of whom had been guillotined. These other leaders were our old friends Billaud Varennes, Collot D'Herbois and Barrére, together with another committee-man, Vadier. A demonstration in their favour, organised by the workmen's faubourgs of St. Antoine and St. Marceau, availed nothing. On 21st March (1st Germinal) they were brought before the Convention, and the proceedings lasted nine days.

Though gallantly defended by the wreck of the Mountain, they were like to be condemned, when once more the loyal workmen's quarters made an attempt to rescue them, and stormed the Convention to the cry of " Bread, the Constitution of '93, and the Liberty of the Patriots!" This, too, proved abortive. Yet possibly fear of popular resentment prevented the Convention from passing a capital sentence this time. It confined itself to condemning the accused to transportation to Cayenne, where Collot took the yellow fever, drank off a whole bottle of brandy, and died; and Billaud amused himself with breeding negroes and tame parrots.

The turn of Fouquier Tinville and the jurymen of the Revolutionary Tribunal came next. They were condemned and executed early in May. " Where are now thy batches?" mockingly exclaimed some of the crowd, as Fouquier mounted the scaffold. " Wretched *canaille,*" replied he, " is your bread any the cheaper for not having

them ? " In truth, the economic situation was fearful.
The abolition of the *maximum* and the forced currency
produced a terrific crisis. The value of 5,000 francs in
paper (assignats) sank to 20 francs in silver or gold. Forestalling, swindling, and extortion of every kind had a
high time of it. Never before had starvation claimed so
many victims as now. Death by the guillotine was succeeded by death from hunger. The crowds at the bakers'
doors were worse than even before the Revolution.
Bitterly did St. Antoine and St. Marceau look back on
the time when, under the Commune and the Committees,
they had a sufficiency and power.

The last of the popular insurrections (unless we in-
clude the abortive Babœuf conspiracy as one) took place
on the 20th May (1st Prairial) of this year, 1795 (111),
and was a well-organised and determined movement, but
lacked leaders and staying power, and consequently fell
through. The chief demands were still "Bread, the
Constitution of '93, the release of all imprisoned patriots!"
The faubourgs this time marched fully armed upon
the Convention, which was taken by surprise, the daily
recurring disturbances having hidden from it the fact
that an organised insurrection was brewing. The doors
were forced, and the *sansculottes* rushed in. At first repulsed, they returned in greater numbers. They fired at
the president, Boissy D'Anglas. A deputy, Féraud, who
rushed forward to protect him, was cut down by sabres,
and his head fixed on a pike. All the deputies now fled,
except those forming the rump of the old Mountain, to
the number of about sixty. Romme (him of the calendar) now took the chair, and all the demands of the insurgents were put and carried in rapid succession.

But the wealthy " sections " had been apprised of what
had happened and had meantime quietly surrounded the
Tuileries. Finally, a drilled body of *Jeunesse Dor e*
suddenly burst in, and drove out the insurgents in confusion at the point of the bayonet. The deputies re-

entered. All the decrees just passed were annulled. The members of the "Mountain" were arrested as accomplices of the insurgents, and secretly conveyed away from Paris. But the *sansculottes* did not consider themselves beaten. Next day they again assembled in the outer faubourgs and proceeded to march on the Convention, this time taking their cannon with them. The inner or wealthy middle-class sections were also drawn up in arms on the Place du Carrousel in defence of the Assembly. The cannon of the faubourgs was already pointed on the Tuileries when the Convention sent commissioners to treat with the insurgents. Their demands were pretended to be favourably received, but nothing was definitely promised. This sufficed, however, to put the *sansculottes* off their guard. Not having an energetic Commune and a determined commander at their back, as on the 31st of May, 1793, they retired satisfied with some vague conciliatory phrases, a course proving fatal to the insurrection which, at the opening of the day, had stood a fair chance of success, and fatal also, as the event showed, to the cause of the democracy.

. A few days later the assassin of Féraud, who had been tried and condemned to death, was on his way to execution when the populace delivered him and carried him in triumph into the faubourgs. The Convention then ordered the latter to be disarmed. The interior sections surrounded the working-class quarters the next day for the purpose of carrying out this decree. After some resistance it was effected. The faubourgs surrendered unconditionally with their arms and cannon.

The Paris working classes were now reduced, therefore, to the condition of an unarmed mob, and for them organised insurrection was a thing of the past. Royalism became again fashionable. It was openly advocated in newspapers and in public assemblies, and even inside the Convention itself, though here it remained in a minority. Meanwhile, the " White Terror " was raging in the provinces far worse than in Paris. The South, especially, became the scene of wholesale massacres of all supposed to be friendly to revolutionary principles. Bands of returned "emigrants" and wealthy young men, called "Companies of Jesus" and "Companies of the Sun," went about killing every Revolutionist, or suspected Revolutionist, they could find. The Jacobins had been arrested wholesale during the last few weeks. The prisons were broken into, and every "sansculotte" massacred. At Lyons 300 Jacobins were enclosed in a shed, which was then set fire to, a cordon being formed round it till they were consumed to a man. At Tarascon hundreds of victims were hurled from the top of a rock into the Rhone. This sort of thing went on for weeks without any attempt to stop it on the part of the authorities. The canting middle-class humbugs who have dilated on the "horrors of the French Revolution" and of the "mob" with so much unction, have prudently passed over the still worse horrors of the Reaction and the "respectable classes." It is noteworthy that many of the most ardent of the Thermidorian reactionaries were precisely men who, a few months previously, had been the most ardent revolutionists, and, in many cases, like Fréron, Fouché, and Tallien, the most truculent agents of the "Terror."

In Paris, encouraged by impunity, the Royalists at last attempted an insurrection against the Convention, finding that they were not likely to obtain a majority in that body. The immediate occasion of it was the conditions under which the Assembly was to be dissolved. The new Constitution which had been voted was very much on the model of that of 1791. A property qualification and indirect voting were, of course, re-introduced, with two Chambers, a Council of 500, and a Senate of 250 members, capped by an Executive Committee or Directory of five, having power to appoint six Ministers. The electoral divisions of France were re-organised in an anti-demoeratic sense. Now, with this constitution, the Royalists hoped to have obtained a majority in the next Parliament, and were grievously disappointed when the Convention enacted that two-thirds of the new body should be chosen from its own members. Hence the tears of the Royalists, and hence the insurrection of the wealthy and well-armed Royalist section against the Convention on the 5th October, 1795 (13th of Vendémiaire, III.), the task of quelling which was entrusted by Barras, the generalissimo of the Convention, to a young artillery officer, Napoleon Bonaparte by name, a task the said young artillery officer duly accomplished by the aid of well-planted cannon on the evening of the same day.

CHAPTER XXIV.

THE BABŒUF CONSPIRACY AND END OF THE FRENCH REVOLUTION.

THE insurrection of Vendémiaire gave a slight check to the reaction which had, up to this time, gone on unimpeded. The majority of the Convention, much as they dreaded a return of real revolutionary government, were too much involved politically and economically in the Revolution to be able to tolerate a complete relapse to the old *régime*. What they desired was a plutocratic Republic, in which money should take the place of privilege, and a wealthy middle-class succeed to the power of the old *noblesse* and the crown. And the new Constitution, with its "council of five hundred," its "senate of ancients," its "directorate," its property qualification, and its indirect suffrage, seemed admirably calculated to ensure this end. On the 26th of October the National Convention proclaimed itself dissolved, after an existence of three years and a month, and the elections were held, and the Directory established shortly after.

One result of the events of the 5th October (13th Vendémiaire) was not unnaturally a greater toleration of the popular party, many of whom had taken up arms on the last-mentioned date against the common enemy, the Royalists. The democrats established a club for purposes of political discussion at the Pantheon, which was, for some time, unmolested by the new Government, *viz.*, the Directory. The leader of the club was Gracchus Babœuf, who obtained the title of "Tribune of the People." He had occupied an obscure Government post during the Terror, but had not hitherto played any important part in the Revolution.

The society at the Pantheon grew daily in numbers, and with it grew the influence of Babœuf. The members at length ventured to repair to their meeting-place in arms, and whispers of a projected insurrection soon made themselves heard. The Directory thereupon became alarmed, and on the 26th of February, 1796 (8th Ventose, IV.), peremptorily closed the Pantheon and forbade any further meetings of the club. The followers of Babœuf, among whom were the remnant of the old Commune and Committees, and of course all the old Jacobins, then resorted to direct conspiracy and managed to win over the "legion of police," but here again they were outwitted by the Directory, which immediately disarmed and disbanded this body. The Babœuvists (as they were called) now assembled secretly in a place they named the "Temple of Reason," and concerted measures for an organised insurrection and attack on the governing bodies. They succeeded in rallying in a short time most of the revolutionary elements of France.

It was agreed to form a new Convention, of which the nucleus was to be such remnant of the old Mountain as death, proscription, and desertion had left. Armed bands were suddenly to march from several points concentrically upon the Directory and councils. The Babœuvists believed themselves sure of the military stationed at the Camp of Grenelle, and an officer named Grisel was in their confidence. Everything was arranged up to the night of the projected movement. Two placards were about to be posted up, one bearing the words, "Constitution of 1793, Liberty, Equality, and general happiness," the other the motto, "Those who usurp supreme power ought to be put to death by freemen," and the signal was agreed upon for action, when the chiefs were suddenly surprised and arrested in their council chamber (May 10th). They had been betrayed by Grisel. Babœuf, while in prison, wrote to the directors suggesting a compromise. He was, nevertheless, with the other leaders sent before the new high court of Vendôme.

On the 7th of September following, while they were still awaiting their trial, their followers, to the number of some hundreds, made an armed attack on the Luxembourg, the palace of the directors, but were repulsed by the guards placed there for its defence. They then proceeded to the camp of Grenelle, in the hope of raising the military, in which they were again unsuccessful, being met by a determined resistance. A sharp skirmish followed, ending in the complete rout of the insurgents, who left a large number of dead on the field. This was the last attempt of the democracy to recover its position.

Almost all the leaders and organisers of the Babœuf movement were executed by the sentence of military commissions, and numbers of other persons were imprisoned and exiled. Babœuf himself, and Darthé, the late secretary of Lebon, after acquitting themselves during their trial in a manly manner, fully avowing their principles, stabbed themselves to death with daggers on hearing their sentence. The objects of Babœuf and his followers were definitely and frankly communistic, which cannot be said of any other of the revolutionary parties. Babœuf himself (who, by the side of Marat, Chaumette, Clootz and Pache, may be regarded as one of the noblest and most disinterested of all the leaders of the time) if, in his theoretical scheme, he was the first of the utopian Socialists, also forestalled in his notion of the necessity of taking possession of the political power, one of the foremost principles of the modern Socialist movement.

With the final extinction of the party of Babœuf in September, 1796, after which the French democracy never again rallied, the French Revolution, as a distinct event in history, may be considered to come to an end. From the meeting of the States-General in May, 1789, to the date just mentioned, was only a little more than seven years, but what an experience France and Europe had passed through. Since Camille Desmoulins delivered his famous harangue in the Palais Royal Gardens on that July day in '89, when revolutionary ardour seemed so single in its purpose—how many parties had been consumed, how many enthusiasms had been burnt out!

With the forlorn attempt of the Babœuvists on Grenelle, revolutionary fervour gasped its last breath. The Bourgeois had conquered; the day of the Proletarian was not yet, in spite of his temporary accession to power during the great revolutionary years.

The events succeeding the collapse of the Babœuf movement may be signalised in a few sentences. The populace of Paris and the other large cities gradually settled down into a private life of toil and hardship, and an indifference to public affairs. The wealthy classes plunged into every form of speculation and extravagance. The new middle-class Republic became apparently every day more consolidated. It flourished at home under the director Barras and his colleagues, of whom Carnot was one, and abroad under its new general, Bonaparte. Conquest again followed conquest. New republics, on the model of the French, sprung up like mushrooms in Holland, Liguria, Lombardy, Sardinia, Switzerland, &c. The fresh elections in May, 1797, nevertheless yielded a royalist majority in the Councils, the upshot of which was that Barras and the majority of the directors by the following September, when things had come to a crisis, had to call in the aid of the army under General Augereau to overawe the legislature. This succeeded, and a large number of members, including some "rats" of the old Dantonist party, were exiled on the ground of Royalist intrigues to overthrow the Republic. Carnot and Barthélemy were driven from the Directory. The latter now became practically a dictatorship, with Barras as head dictator.

Most of the powers, tired of prosecuting an adverse war, were glad to make terms of peace. England was soon the only belligerent remaining. But the Directory, without money, and having only the armies to fall back upon, could not afford to bring about a complete cessation of hostilities. Bonaparte, after having subdued the Continent, about this time returned to Paris, the most popular man in France. Barras, feeling his presence dangerous at home, invited him at once to undertake the task of subduing the British power. He readily acceded, and the brilliant Egyptian campaign entered upon with a view to India, was the result. The elections of 1798, which were, unlike those of the previous year, too radical to please the Directory, were annulled, but those of the following year, 1799, yielded the same result.

Meanwhile a new coalition had been formed, one of the principal factors of which was Russia. The unpopular Directory could no longer hold out against public opinion. Negotiations between the various parties were entered into without issue, and the government at home was in great confusion when Bonaparte suddenly appeared on the scene, having left his Oriental army in the hands of General Kléber. A conspiracy was at once formed, led by the old Constitutionalist, Siéyès, to place dictatorial authority in the hands of the successful general. The Senate, seduced by the report of a pretended Jacobin insurrection in the departments, which was to shortly reach Paris, consented to decree the removal of both houses of legislature to the palace of St. Cloud, near Paris, and to placing Bonaparte at the head of the military forces of the capital.

This was on the 9th November, 1799 (18th Brumaire, VII.). The following day the legislature removed to St. Cloud. The "Council of Ancients" met in the "Gallery of Mars," one of the apartments of the Palace, and the council of five hundred in the "Orangery." The "Council of Five Hundred" unanimously swore to the existing Constitution, refusing to ratify the powers given by the other body. Bonaparte was driven away with cries of " Down with the tyrant !" &c. His brother, Lucien Bonaparte, who was president, finding nothing was to be done, came out and harangued the troops, stating that the Assembly was being intimidated by a minority of the members with drawn daggers. Bonaparte, thus fortified, then gave orders for the " Orangery " to be cleared by the military, which was immediately effected. Thus was the Consulate founded. From this to the consecration as Emperor in 1804 was but a step.

CHAPTER XXV

THE course of the Revolution cannot be properly estimated without taking into consideration the results of the confiscation of the property of the nobility and clergy. In the Directoral Constitution of 1795 (III.) we read, Article 374: "The French nation proclaims, as guarantee of public faith, that after an adjudication legally consummated, of the national goods, whatever may be its origin, the legitimate acquirer thereof cannot be dispossessed." The same clause, but slightly modified, is introduced into the Consular Constitution of 1800 (VIII.), and the Imperial Constitution of 1804 (XII.). There is more than meets the eye in these articles. They are the issue and sanction of a series of transactions which established a wealthy plutocracy on the ruins of the old feudal aristocracy of France.

The first property to be sold was that of the Church. This, which in a sense may be considered as having been held in trust for the poor, was primarily disposed of, not to benefit them, but to reduce the public debt and preserve the State from financial ruin. The sales began in 1789, and the period of greatest activity was from August, 1790, to January, 1791. French companies, English companies, Dutch companies, disputed for the spoil, only a comparatively few lots falling to the share of the peasantry, since no restriction was laid on the amount sold to any one purchaser. The sales were the more easily effected, inasmuch as only a small percentage of the purchase-money had to be paid down. When the time came for the second instalment, the money for payment was, naturally, considering the vast extent of the purchases, in most cases not available. This led many of the speculators to favour the Revolution, and all of them to urge on the foreign war, both of which would serve as an excuse for postponement. War was accordingly proclaimed in April, 1792, and the following August the throne was overturned. After the latter event it was decided that the lands and property of the emigrant aristocrats which now came into the market should not be sold hap-hazard and *en masse* like the ecclesiastical property, but should be duly apportioned into small lots, which the small cultivator might hire or purchase on easy terms.

This concession on the part of the middle classes was, however, simply the result of fear of imminent foreign invasion. No sooner had the armies of Dumouriez driven the enemy back than the new Assembly, the Convention, announced that the partition of the public lands must be indefinitely postponed on account of the difficulty of the operation. During the winter '92-3 the moveable effects of the "emigrants" came into the possession of speculators and jobbers by means of sham sales. So flagrant was the abuse, that the Convention had to step in, but without much effect. After the fall of the Girondists the partition of the lands among the peasantry was again definitely ordered. The second grand campaign now intervened, and France was for the moment converted into one vast camp. Exceptional measures were the order of things all round, and comparatively few small transfers were effected. This did not prevent the confiscation both of the lands and moveables of the nobles and suspects going on at a greater pace than ever. But it was various agents of the Government in the departments who made vast fortunes out of them by their clever manœuvring. Two-thirds of the houses in Paris were now "national property." The Convention decreed that "goods" to the value of one milliard should be reserved for the citizen soldiers returned from the wars. This milliard, we need scarcely say, remained a promise to the end of the chapter.

The Committee of Public Safety, early in '94, ordered the sale of the confiscated lands to be proceeded with, but while recommending that the principle of partition should be adopted, did not insist upon it, the net result of the new sales being that large tracts of public land were sold in the lump as before, but this time they went into the possession of a new class of thieves; to wit, the victuallers of the armies, who had already made large fortunes out of their contracts. After Thermidor, this, of course, went forward on a larger scale than ever.

Robespierre, through his agent, St. Just, now got a decree passed that indigent patriots should be indemnified out of the goods of the "enemies of the Revolution," but this decree was merely procured to maintain his popularity with the people, as was proved by the fact that he never so much as attempted to put it into execution.

The 9th of Thermidor arrived without the working-classes of the towns having touched any of the "goods" of the emigrants, the clergy, or the suspects, while the peasantry had to be satisfied with here and there a few crumbs in the shape of the partition of communal lands. Barrére had said that they had coined money on the Place de la Revolution, but the working-classes can certainly not be accused of having shared in this ill-gotten gain. Thus, even while the masses were nominally in power, the middle-classes succeeded in "nobling" the Revolution.

After the insurrection of Thermidor, the traffic in the "national property" proceeded more unblushingly than ever. As soon as the *maximum* was abolished, however, the plutocracy found even it more to their interest for the moment to *hocus* the currency than to purchase land, at however reduced a money value. By procuring a practically unlimited issue of paper they succeeded in reducing the value of the *assignats* to next to nothing. The forestalling of the necessaries of life, especially grain, which was the immediate cause of the various insurrections after Thermidor up to that of Babœuf, was also a stupendous source of profit. The re-opening of the Bourse, the repudiation of the hypothec of the *assignats* on the confiscated lands, the latter a piece of thieving of the most impudent character, followed in the natural course of things. Lotteries were instituted, the prizes of which were the " national property." One deputy even had the impudence to propose to take back the lands already distributed amongst the peasantry. But this was thought to be too risky. Meanwhile, the victories of the armies under Bonaparte opened fresh fields and pastures new for every form of swindling by means of provisioning "contracts." A cessation of the war would, indeed, have been a grievous thing for the rising plutocracy of France. Under the Directory the exploiters flung themselves anew upon the as yet undisturbed territories. Everything was now in their own hands. No stone was left unturned to diminish for the nonce the market value of this property. The price which was paid in depreciated ·paper taken at the nominal value was in most cases simply farcical.

But all means of robbery were not yet exhausted. The army contractors refused to be paid any longer in *assignats*, but insisted on large sums being placed to their credit in the books of the national debt, thus saddling themselves in perpetuity on the French people. Deputies, Government-agents, generals, contractors, engaged in a mad scramble which could make the most out of the situation. The masses of France had but two purposes in their eyes—to labour at home at starvation wages, insufficient to support life for any but the strongest, and to serve as food for powder abroad. The vast territorial estates of the feudal aristocracy, and the house property of the towns, thus passed into the hands of another and a meaner set of lords, The new middle-class of France was consolidated economically and politically. Verily the French Revolution was a success—for them! And now having reached the summit of their ambition, it only remained to kick over the ladder which had helped them up. The hearth, the throne, and the altar must be re-established on a new basis; we must have done with revolution and all its wicked ways! said they. Revolution must be henceforth a thing accursed! But a Republic, no matter how safeguarded against intrusion of the "common people," seemed to many an insufficient guarantee under the existing circumstances for the newly created "order." A military dictator, who knew how to smother insurrections in the birth, he was the man for the situation, and his name was—Napoleon Bonaparte.

CHAPTER XXVI.

CONCLUSION.

THE French Revolution closes in a final and definite manner an epoch in the world's history. The middle ages, proper, it is true, came to an end with the 16th century. But they left a kind of afterglow behind them in the shape of the centralised and quasi-absolute princedoms and monarchies which prevailed during the 17th and 18th centuries; in the continuance in rural districts and the smaller towns of the old methods of industry but slightly, if at all, modified; in the perpetuation unabated, for over a century at least, of mediæval and renaissance superstitions and habits of thought; in short, in the survival of most of the external forms of the old-world civilisation, decayed like the foliage of a St. Martin's summer. The conversion of the feudal hierarchies into centralised monarchies but imperfectly freed the middle classes; the combined or workshop system of production had not in any marked or violent manner revolutionised industry; the learning of the renaissance had, to a large extent, merely given a quasi-scientific and systematic shape to old habits of thought.

The political, moral and social changes leading up to modern times were of course going on all the while, and were observable to the truly observant, but were not at that time of a " run and read " character.

The French Revolution definitely closes this epoch. It does even more. It constitutes the dividing line between the world of to-day and all past ages whatever. The Revolution was scarcely over when the electric telegraph appeared on the scene. At the same time the idea of the steam engine was working in the heads of the ingenious, and the closing years of the century saw the first of the new industrial machines established in the factories of the North of England. New stage-coach roads, canals, and other "improvements" sprang up in all directions. A couple of decades or so more and the great industry was to start the metamorphosis of human production and distribution; yet another, and the railway was to begin the transformation of the face of nature and the externals of human life in other directions. In short, from the French Revolution we advance straight by leaps and bounds to the modern world.

The city of Paris well typifies the progress. One hundred years ago, in 1789, it was (unlike London, which in its mediæval form was destroyed by the fire of 1666), to all intents and purposes a mediæval city, substantially the Paris of Victor Hugo's "Notre Dame," a city of feudal fortresses, high-walled enclosures, crooked, narrow, unpaved streets. The Committee of Public Safety in 1793 began alterations, partly with a view of giving employment to distressed workmen. The changes went on gradually, till, in 1859, Haussmann, under Napoleon III., totally destroyed what remained of old Paris, and laid out the city in the form we see it to-day—a city which would be as foreign to Danton, Robespierre, or Marat as San Francisco itself. The Paris of centuries perished in little more than fifty years. What is true of Paris is true of Europe—of the whole of existing civilisation. The Europe of 1789 was in the main the Europe of the later middle ages—of the renaissance—but in the last stage of decay. It had been practically dead for over two centuries, and like Edgar Poe's hypnotised dead man, it fell to pieces with a sudden convulsive awaking after proclaiming itself dead. No "restoration" could really bring it together again. The new world of our time had, meanwhile, grown up, with its science, its inventions, its

intense self-consciousness, and placed insurmountable
barriers between us and our naïve and simple-minded
ancestors. The old Merry England, for example, the England of the fairy ring and the Maypole, had passed away
for ever. In politics the reign of the bourgeoisie with
its oppression resting on cunning and hypocrisy had
shut out the possibility of an enduring reaction to the
coarser and more direct methods of feudal domination.

There are several minor points worthy of notice afforded
by the course of the French Revolution. One feature of
the period, already alluded to, its perpetual reference to
classical models, and its somewhat mechanical attempt to
make history repeat itself—to reproduce the Republics of
ancient Greece and Rome in eighteenth-century France—
can never be left out of sight. Every man's head was
full of "Plutarch's Lives." All men, however little else they
knew, seem to have had at least a superficial schoolboy
smattering of Roman history. Almost every speech and
every newspaper article of the time bristles with references to Coriolanus, Cato, Cicero, Brutus, or Cæsar. In
fact, Roman history was to the French Revolution very
much what the Jewish annals, contained in the Bible,
were to the English rebellion under Charles I. "We," or
rather modern science and historical criticism, "have
changed all that." We no longer look to the past as a
model for the society of the present or the future. The
doctrine of evolution has taught us that human society,
like everything else, is a growth, and that though corresponding and analogous phases certainly do recur in
history, we can yet never argue back from one period to
another, as though there had been no intervening devel-
opment, or as though the economical, intellectual, and
political conditions were substantially the same, or might
be made the same.

Another point the Revolution teaches us is the effective power of minorities. The Terror itself (whatever
view we may take as to its justifiability), it cannot be

denied, was kept up for nearly two years by a comparatively small but energetic minority in all the towns of France. Outside this minority (the Jacobins) there was a floating mass of inert sympathy with the objects of Sansculottism, and a belief in the necessity of drastic measures in view of the situation. Beyond this, again, was the vast mass of inert stupidity and indifference which was effectually cowed. The active enemies of the Revolution were, of course, reduced to silence.

It is significant, again, to notice that most of the great crises were connected with affairs on the frontiers. The 10th of August and the September massacres were the response to Brunswick's manifesto, and the march of the enemy on the capital respectively. The 31st of May was directly brought about by the invasion of the new coalition and the disorganisation of Dumouriez's armies, consequent on his defection. Finally, the 9th of Thermidor, and the abolition of the "Terror," followed on the disappearance of the last trace of danger from the foreigner consequent on the battle of Fleurus.

The extraordinary enthusiasm which we find, the reckless readiness of all alike to inflict and to suffer death, might lead us to suppose the men of the time to have been a race of born heroes, or monsters, or both. The average of them were neither the one nor the other. They were the products of social forces beyond their control. The feeling of the all-importance of the public interest carried all before it. Prior to the Revolution, they were probably neither more courageous nor more truculent than ourselves. The same courage and the same truculency might manifest itself in any man of character under like circumstances. Even Robespierre was, as Carlyle suggests, probably neither better nor worse than other attorneys to start with. But in his case ambition ultimately assumed the mastery over his whole personality. This was partly owing to the fact that he was undeniably a man without a vice (in the

ordinary sense of the word). Now only very exceptional
men can afford to be without the ordinary vices of man-
kind, and Robespierre was certainly not one of these
men. With his ascetic Rousseauite notions of republican
austerity, he had suppressed his natural appetites, the
consequence being that all the morbid elements in his
character, having no other outlet, ran into the channel of
self-idolatry and morbid ambition. The first condition
of a well-regulated man is to know how to properly
distribute the *quantum* of vice with which a bountiful
nature has endowed him. A false morality teaches him
to suppress it. But this he can seldom do, and if he
succeeds, it is at the expense of all or much that is dis-
tinctive in his character. In tearing off the coating of
vice, he tears off his skin with it. The usual case, however, is that the vice is not got rid of at all, but only
forced into some out-of-the-way channel. And whenever
vice is concentrated, it is bad. When all the vice of a
character is focussed on any single one of the natural
appetites, a man becames a sot, a satyr, a glutton, a
confirmed gambler, &c. Now Robespierre sat upon all
the usual valves. He and his ascetic band poured scorn
on the Hébertists and the Dantonists alike for the "loose-
ness" of their lives. But having closed up all the
ordinary exits, his vice came out none the less, but concentrated in the form of a truculent, remorseless ambition,
unparalleled in history.

The rank and file of the actors in the Revolution it is
difficult, for the reasons before stated, to characterise by
any of the ordinary ethical standards. The best of them
did things we cannot always approve while sitting com-
fortably in our chairs, the worst of them showed much
genuine and disinterested devotion to the cause of the
people. Were we called upon to name the five men
whose aims were probably the purest, we would mention
Marat, Chaumette, Clootz, Pache and Babœuf. Danton,
apart from the disputed question of his bribery, was a

mere politician, who only interested himself in social questions, when at all, in so far as they immediately affected the political situation.

The issue of the French Revolution was, as we have seen, the modern world of great capital and free trade, as opposed to the old world of land and privilege and all that that change implies. In the storm and stress of outward events, we are apt to forget the work done during the Terror era by the committees of the Convention—administrative, educational, and legal work, which helped to build up the modern governmental system. The "Code Napoleon" itself was based on the labour of Merlin de Douai and his committee. In France, the political and juridical side of the great change was most prominent; in Germany, the philosophical and literary; in England, the industrial and commercial. While French politicians were engaged in establishing the Republic, German thinkers were engaged in founding 19th century thought, and English inventors in establishing the new modes of production and locomotion. But while the mediæval organisation of society held together for centuries, the modern is already showing signs of approaching disintegration. Why is this? We answer, because the latter contained, from the first, in its very nature, the seeds of dissolution. The capitalistic system of necessity feeds upon itself. Competition, which is the breath of its life, necessarily also destroys that life. It may be that the "opening up" of Africa, and other as yet unexploited territories, will give the system a further lease of existence, lasting some decades, but the end cannot in any case be a long by-and-by.

THE END.

Printed by Cowan & Co., Limited, Perth.

INDEX.

1

www.ingramcontent.com/pod-product-compliance
Lightning Source LLC
Chambersburg PA
CBHW032012010726
47493CB00007B/2361